"While we're talking a said, "let me say I thou was a nice idea."

"You did? How'd you know al

"You mean, how did I know about it since I didn't get one in my box?"

Sunni looked guilty.

"You forget, Ms. Vanderclef—I know everything."

"That's right. You did mention principals are omniscient."

the
ca   s you
ma

T   sad.
his   ut of
a g   have
loc   d to

                                                              bout
wi

                                                              your
mind."

As she reached for the door, he said, "Wait. Haven't we forgotten something?"

"What's that?"

"My professional advice for the day.

"Okay. What is it?"

"Keep up the good work."

NANCY LAVO married her college sweetheart, and they have been blessed with three wonderful children and a terrific son-in-law. They all make their homes in the great state of Texas. For fun, Nancy takes long walks with her husband, meets friends for lunch, or muddles through crossword puzzles. Occasionally she sits down and writes a book. *Miss Menace* is Nancy's fifth book for Heartsong Presents.

Books by Nancy Lavo

HEARTSONG PRESENTS
HP133—Change of Heart
HP179—Father's Love
HP250—Something from Nothing
HP388—Lessons in Love

Don't miss out on any of our super romances. Write to us at the following address for information on our newest releases and club information.

Heartsong Presents Readers' Service
PO Box 721
Uhrichsville, OH 44683

Or visit www.heartsongpresents.com

Miss Menace

Nancy Lavo

Heartsong Presents

To the Ladies Who Lunch:

   Debra, Jill, Kathy, Nancy, and Vicki.

   What a blessing you are in my life. " 'I thank my God upon every remembrance of you' " (Philippians 1:3).

A note from the Author:
I love to hear from my readers! You may correspond with me by writing:

Nancy Lavo
Author Relations
PO Box 721
Uhrichsville, OH 44683

ISBN 1-59310-849-4

MISS MENACE

Our mission is to publish and distribute inspirational products offering exceptional value and biblical encouragement to the masses.

Cover design by Jocelyne Bouchard

PRINTED IN THE U.S.A.

one

Sunni Vanderclef never met a man she didn't like. Until today. Here she was within a millimeter of detesting Ethan Harris, and they'd only just met.

He wasn't a bad-looking man. In fact, he was gorgeous. Tall and tan with thick, wavy brown hair and a killer physique, Ethan Harris looked more like a hunky soap opera star than a middle school principal.

He'd be the stuff dreams were made of if it weren't for the cynical expression currently marring his handsome face.

"Tell me about yourself, Ms. Vanderclef." He wasn't asking her; he was challenging her.

She couldn't imagine why, but it was obvious he didn't like her. She sat up a little straighter. No way was she going to let him intimidate her. She wanted the job.

She flashed him a brilliant smile, determined to wow him with her kindness. She injected an extra dose of perkiness into her voice and said, "I'm Sunni Vanderclef—that's Sunni with an 'i'—and I'm twenty-five years old. I received my degree in education from Baylor University."

He lifted his eyes from her application to look at her. "It says here you graduated three years ago. What have you been doing since then?"

Hmm. Tough question.

She knew he wasn't impressed with her elementary education credentials. She wished she could tell him she'd spent

5

the past three years teaching orphans in a third world country or organizing a chain of food banks across the metroplex.

Unfortunately it wasn't true. And Sunni Vanderclef wasn't a liar. Still, it was a shame. He was obviously expecting the worst, and she hated to deliver.

"I've been tied up with pressing social obligations."

He cocked a dark, mocking brow. "Is that right?"

She nodded. "I have lots of family responsibilities. Not that I have my own family. Not yet." Her smile faltered. "I'm single."

And that, she thought, *is the whole problem.* If she were married as she was supposed to be, she wouldn't be sitting across the desk from Ethan the Evil.

Though never officially engaged, Sunni knew she and Mason would marry. After meeting in her church's college group, they'd been dating steadily since her senior year at Baylor. They were perfect for each other. Everyone said so.

Sunni was still reeling from their conversation last night. She'd nearly fainted when faithful Mason looked into her eyes and told her he was engaged to a girl he'd met at his office.

Stunned, Sunni had asked, "But what does she have that I don't have?"

Mason had smiled the lovesick smile formerly reserved for Sunni and said, "Ashley is different. She's serious. She wants to make something of her life. I realized she's the kind of person I want to spend the rest of my life with."

Sunni shook her head to dispel the memory. She couldn't believe it. She wouldn't believe it. Mason was hers. He just didn't know it.

Ethan Harris rested his elbows on the desk and peered at

her over his steepled fingers. "I'm curious. How did you find out about our opening here?"

Glad to be off the painful flashback of Mason, Sunni's smile was back in full force. "I stopped by the elementary school to pick up an employment application, and they told me there was an opening in the home economics department at the middle school."

"If I read this application correctly, it says you are an elementary education major. Do you know anything about home ec, Ms. Vanderclef?"

She flipped her hair back off her shoulder. "Oh, sure. I'm totally into nutrition. And I can cook," she threw in as a bonus.

"Is that right?"

Did the man have only one tone—sarcastic? She pressed on, determined not to let him get to her. "Absolutely. I know it's tacky to brag, but my chocolate chip cookies were the talk of the campus."

He gave her a long, hard look before sitting back in his chair and studying her application. Sunni watched the seconds tick by on the big round clock hanging on the wall behind him.

Finally he took a deep breath and lowered the forms. "I'm in a bind."

He swiveled to look over his shoulder at the clock she'd been watching. "It's four fifteen on Friday. School starts Monday morning at eight o'clock sharp, and I don't have a home ec teacher. Since I didn't need a home ec teacher until today at nine when my current teacher drove her car into the back of an eighteen-wheeler and broke her arm, both legs, and an as-yet-undetermined number of ribs, I haven't had time to interview candidates for the job. Yours is the only application."

She grinned at what was clearly God's answer to her desperate prayer that morning. "That should make your decision easy."

He wasn't amused. "Unfortunately it does not. You see, you are not what I am looking for."

Her brows shot up. "Not one for beating around the bush, are you?"

"I don't have time for anything but plain speaking. I have a school to run and a reputation to maintain. Central Middle School is one of a handful in the entire state to be designated as a Blue Ribbon school. To maintain that top rating, I need a staff of committed professionals, not socialites who decide to set aside their 'pressing social obligations' to play schoolteacher."

Sunni sucked in a shocked breath. How dare he dismiss her life so casually? If she didn't need the job so badly, she'd have cheerfully crawled over the desk and slapped his self-righteous face. But if she was going to prove to Mason and the rest of the world that she was serious, she needed a job. And the home ec position at the middle school was the district's only opening for which she was even remotely qualified.

"I didn't apply for the job so I could play teacher. I applied for the job because I want to work. I may not be your dream applicant, but it's now four twenty-six on Friday afternoon, and I'm all you've got. It strikes me that a socialite for a teacher beats no teacher at all."

He must have seen the reason in what she said, but he obviously didn't like it. "I suppose you're better than nothing."

"Thank you," she said, ignoring the insult. "I'd like to think so."

He sighed. "All right, Ms. Vanderclef. You're hired. But I'm offering you only a conditional contract."

"A trial basis?"

"That's right. Before I issue you a full year's contract, you have to prove yourself. Is that a problem?"

She thrust her chin up. "Not at all. I look forward to it."

Ethan Harris was on his feet, with the first pleasant expression she'd seen on his face. It was fairly insulting to realize the only way she could bring a smile to his face was by leaving.

"Excellent," he said. "That concludes our business." He extended his arm toward the door. "If you will step outside my office, my secretary, Mrs. Leeper, will give you the necessary paperwork and fill you in on our schedule for the next few days."

"Thank you." Sunni strode out with her head high.

Mrs. Leeper was as nice as Mr. Harris was nasty. Totally gray and comfortably plump, she reminded Sunni of a kindly grandmother. "So you're going to be working here at Central." She beamed at Sunni. "That's just lovely. It's always good to add a new face to the staff. Especially one as pretty as yours."

"Thank you." Sunni wondered how Ethan the Ogre kept such a treasure in his employment. He probably chained her to the desk. She peeked over the desk, looking for manacles.

Mrs. Leeper grew serious. She lowered her voice. "Since you are going to work here, I probably ought to warn you about the football coach, Jerry Rawley. He's single and, from what I hear, quite the ladies' man."

Touched by her concern, Sunni nodded solemnly. "I'll be careful."

"Good girl." Mrs. Leeper pulled several forms from a file on her desk. "Go ahead and fill these out, and I'll carry them over to the district office so they can do a background check on you and get you on the payroll."

Sunni completed the forms and returned them to Mrs. Leeper. "That's it? I'm a teacher?" For all her brave talk, she was worried. "I don't even know where my classroom is."

"Don't worry," Mrs. Leeper said. "Mr. Harris is holding a meeting tomorrow morning for all the new and returning teachers. Afterward, you'll have time to tour the school and settle into your classroom."

Sunni frowned. She'd had the job less than ten minutes, and it was already interfering with her social life. "A meeting tomorrow? On a Saturday? What time?"

"Ten o'clock sharp. Mr. Harris is a real stickler for punctuality."

❧

Ethan scrubbed his hands over his face. He'd done it. For better or worse, he'd hired little Miss Sunshine. He couldn't shake the feeling that it was for the worst.

He glanced down at her application. Sunni Vanderclef. He hadn't realized that anyone over the age of sixteen dotted her i's with a heart. He supposed when you came from the kind of money she did, anything goes.

His eyes traveled down the neatly printed page. It said she'd attended Hillcrest Prep School from kindergarten through the twelfth grade. No surprises there. Vanderclefs had been attending that prestigious school since the beginning of time. If he remembered correctly, a half dozen buildings scattered across the century-old campus bore the name *Vanderclef.* More surprising was her showing up at Central Middle today. He'd guess this was the first time a Vanderclef ever set foot in a public school building. Why did it have to be his?

He didn't want her. He'd meant what he said when he told her she wasn't what he was looking for. He needed hard-working teachers—men and women who loved kids enough to want to make a difference in their lives, not frivolous debutantes who thought it might be fun to take a break from partying to play school.

"Pressing social obligations"? Did she honestly think he was stupid enough to believe she'd spent the last three years doing something worthwhile? Or maybe she thought principals didn't read the social pages where her name figured prominently at least three times a week. "SUNNI VANDERCLEF HOSTS A PARTY". . ."VANDERCLEF NAMED CHAIRMAN OF COMMITTEE."

He rolled his eyes. Pressing social obligations. That was nothing more than a fancy way of saying running her legs off flitting from store to store, party to party. He knew the type well. Well enough to know Sunni Vanderclef was not what he was looking for.

Kristen Hobart, the teacher Ms. Vanderclef was to replace, was a principal's dream. A team player and competent teacher, Kristen was always available to help out. If he needed a club sponsor, she'd take the job. When he asked for volunteers to chaperone an event, her hand was always the first one in the air. Kristen was the perfect employee and a good friend. And on the injured list for six months.

No way a twenty-five-year-old sorority girl in a high-priced suit could take Kristen's place.

Ethan buried his face in his hands to pray. "Lord, I asked You for a teacher, and You sent me a socialite. Don't get me wrong, Father. I mean no disrespect when I say I think You missed on this one." He sighed. "I guess I'll have to take it on faith. If You have something to teach me with this, I'm willing to learn. Even so, I want You to know I only hired her to ensure a warm body in front of the home ec class Monday morning and to buy time while I interview more appropriate candidates. I'm not planning on Sunni Vanderclef's being my problem for long."

two

Sunni swung into the school parking lot and parked her sports car in the last available space. She flipped down her visor to check her hair and reapply her lipstick before grabbing her purse and heading to the front doors.

The going was tough in stiletto heels, but knowing the shoes made her outfit, she suffered with a smile on her face. She popped her head into the front office where she could see Mrs. Leeper working at her desk.

"Good morning, Mrs. Leeper. Where's the meeting?"

Mrs. Leeper's good-natured smile morphed into a look of alarm. "You're just getting here? It's almost eleven o'clock, dear. The meeting started an hour ago."

Sunni shrugged. "I know. I had something I had to do first."

"Oh, my." Mrs. Leeper wrung her hands. "What will Mr. Harris say?"

Sunni batted away her concern with a flick of her hand. "Don't worry. Just tell me where they are. I'll slip in the back. Nobody will notice I'm a little bit late."

Mrs. Leeper didn't look convinced. "They're in the library. Down B Hall, second door on the left."

"B Hall, second door on the left. Gotcha." Sunni turned to leave. "Thanks, Mrs. Leeper. See you later."

By reading the names painted on the walls, Sunni was able to locate B Hall. There was the library, two doors down, just

13

as Mrs. Leeper said. Unfortunately Sunni could find only one door leading in.

She slowly pulled open the door and peeked her head inside. *Wouldn't you know it?* She'd entered at the front, three feet from where Mr. Harris was standing. "Oops."

He glared at her. "Welcome, Ms. Vanderclef. Nice of you to join us."

She gave a nervous laugh. "Sorry," she said to both Mr. Harris and the group of teachers seated around tables. "I'll just slip into the back. Forget you even see me. Just continue on with whatever you were doing."

The tap-tap of her heels on the tile floor was the only sound as she walked to an empty chair at a table in the back of the room. She smiled and nodded to the other three occupants before sitting.

She placed her purse on the table just so, scooted her chair to a better angle to see Mr. Harris, and after smoothing her hair, folded her hands in her lap and directed her attention to the podium.

"All settled, Ms. Vanderclef?" Mr. Harris asked in a voice of ominous calm.

She flashed him a bright smile. "Yes, thank you."

"That's just fine. Now, if there are no more interruptions, we will continue. Turn to page 15 in your syllabus. Let me take a minute to go over the policy changes for the coming year."

Sunni glanced at the syllabus sitting at her place before turning her attention to her fellow teachers. Her first impression: She was overdressed. Her darling slim white ankle-length pants and off-the-shoulder sweater looked out of place in a room full of faded T-shirts and jeans. She frowned. Teachers must have changed a lot since she went to school.

The attractive young woman at the table beside Sunni scribbled something on a piece of paper and discreetly slid it to Sunni.

Hi, the note said. *You must be new. I'm Jennifer Stanton, the science teacher.*

Sunni wrote back, *I'm Sunni Vanderclef. Very new. I was hired on Friday afternoon as a home ec teacher.*

Jennifer wrote, *Welcome aboard. Nobody must have told you Harris is a demon for punctuality.*

Sunni answered, *I think Mrs. Leeper mentioned it. Did he look very angry when I walked in?*

Jennifer read the note and nodded before replying, *Major understatement. He looked homicidal.*

Sunni shrugged and wrote, *So what's new? I think the man has hostility issues.*

Jennifer shook her head. *No way. The guy's a teddy bear. Everybody loves him.* She waggled her eyebrows at Sunni as she slid her the note.

It would take more than good looks to make Mr. Disagreeable appeal to her. Sunni snorted and wrote, *Love Mr. Harris? I'll pass.*

After Jennifer read the note, their gazes met, and they started snickering. Both women ducked behind upraised syllabi for cover.

Evidently they weren't as discreet as they thought. Mr. Harris stopped what he was doing. "It's nice to know the district policies on discipline are so amusing. Or maybe you have a joke you'd like to share, Ms. Vanderclef."

Sunni felt as she had in high school when she'd been

caught talking in class. Her face flaming, she said, "No, sir. I've never been good at telling jokes."

"That's too bad. But if you have nothing to share, maybe you'll allow me to finish."

Sunni resisted the temptation to roll her eyes. This guy was such a grump. Mason had better appreciate what she was going through for him. She smiled around gritted teeth. "Please do."

After Mr. Harris finished going through the material in the syllabus, he said, "Monday morning, we begin a new year. It'll take all of you, working as a team, giving it your all, to make it our best year ever. I'm counting on you." He laid the papers on his podium. "That concludes my portion of the meeting. Feel free to go home if you don't have anything left to do in your rooms."

There was a lot of chattering and scraping of chair legs as the faculty got to their feet.

"Oh," Mr. Harris called out over the noise. "I forgot to mention we have a new member on staff. Sunni Vanderclef will be taking Kristen's place in home ec."

That's it? No nice introduction or warm words of welcome? He mentioned her as an afterthought. Was there ever a ruder man?

She didn't have time to sulk. Jennifer extended her hand. "We'll make this official. I'm Jennifer Stanton."

Sunni liked her already. Jennifer looked to be the same age as Sunni, a pretty woman with long red hair pulled back into a ponytail, a ratty Central Middle School T-shirt and jeans, and pink plastic flip-flops. The notes they exchanged were promising, but it was the hot pink polish on Jennifer's toenails that told Sunni they were going to be good friends.

"I'm glad to meet you. You don't look like any science teacher I ever had. Mine were always scary looking, with hunched shoulders and long white lab coats."

Jennifer chuckled. "If you think I look out of character, you should see my fiancé. He teaches high school science and looks like a California surfer."

"I can't wait to meet him."

Several of the other teachers wandered over to Sunni to introduce themselves. Mr. Bewley who taught algebra and couldn't be too many years from retirement, Mrs. Petty who taught English, and a half-dozen others whose names and faces all ran together in Sunni's mind.

"Don't worry," Jennifer whispered. "Give it two weeks, and you'll know everybody and everything there is to know about Central."

"I'd settle for knowing where my classroom is."

"I'll be glad to show you. Come on."

Sunni watched for landmarks as she followed Jennifer down B Hall, left into Hall Two, and left again into the home ec room. Jennifer flipped on the lights. "Here you are. Home sweet home."

Sunni looked around the enormous room with a sense of wonder. Having never taken a home ec class in her life, she had no idea what to expect.

The room was rectangular, wider than it was deep. Divided into thirds, the two outside thirds consisted of three finger-like kitchens jutting out from each outside wall. She counted a total of six kitchens, each equipped with an oven, cook top, and refrigerator, all connected by oak cabinets. The center third of the classroom that ran between the kitchens was a straight shot of desks, four across and six deep.

Sunni did the math and swallowed hard. "Twenty-four students?"

Jennifer nodded. "Yeah, they keep the home ec classes small."

Small? Sunni gulped again. When she was in school, most of her classes had fewer than twenty students. She'd done her student teaching in a kindergarten class of fifteen.

Jennifer walked over to the teacher's desk, a large blond wood desk from the LBJ era, and picked up a piece of paper. "You need to fill this out today. It's a requisition list for supplies you want for the first semester."

"I have no idea what I want."

"Don't panic. I'm sure Kristen's got the kitchens all stocked, and there's plenty of paper and stuff. This is for any personal preferences."

"Like what?" Sunni asked. "What did you order?"

Jennifer thought a moment. "A cat skeleton, a fresh supply of fetal pigs, and a wooden stool."

Sunni shuddered. "Ugh. I'm sorry I asked. I can't imagine I'll be needing cat bones or dead pigs."

"Probably true, but a stool might come in handy."

Sunni looked at the perfectly good chair behind her desk. "What would I do with a stool?"

"Sit on it. To lecture. It puts you up high for maximum visibility in front of the class and gives you a break from standing on your feet all day."

Sunni tried to imagine herself lecturing and decided a stool would be very cool. It seemed like a "teachery" thing to do. She took the paper from Jennifer and wrote *stool*. "What else do I want?"

Jennifer looked around. "I can't think of anything. Kristen

has the place finished out." She walked to the desk and slid open the top drawer. "You've got scissors, paper clips, red pens, and sticky notes. Looks to me like you're ready to go."

"I don't feel ready to go."

Jennifer patted her on the back. "That's new-teacher nerves talking. I had them bad my first year. Give yourself a week or two to get acclimated, and this place will feel like home."

Sunni looked around the dull beige room with its tacky calico-covered bulletin boards and plastic potted plants and doubted very much this place would ever feel like home. "Thanks."

"No problem. Hey, if you're okay, I need to run. I'm supposed to meet my fiancé for lunch. You're welcome to join us if you like."

"No, I ought to hang around here for a while and try to sort things out. But thanks."

"Another time then," Jennifer called over her shoulder as she walked to the door. "See you Monday."

Sunni slumped into the old wooden swivel chair with a ruffled pink calico cushion and propped her elbows on the desk. "O Lord," she prayed, "what have I gotten myself into? Help me."

She wasn't a teacher; she knew nothing about kids. What was she going to do with twenty-four of them assigned to her care?

She tried to cheer herself with memories of her student-teaching days. They'd been fun. The kids had been adorable with their big hair bows and ruffled socks. And she thought they'd liked her. They were always fighting over who could sit next to her during story time or who could hold her hand on the way out to recess.

The memories cheered her. She could do this. She just needed to add a few personal touches to the classroom to make it feel more like home. She'd brought a box of things from her student-teaching days. She'd run out to her car to get them.

Sunni stepped into the hall, once again looking for landmarks to find her way back. She took a left out of her door and a quick right into Hall Two. When she passed the gymnasium, she realized she was lost.

"Well, hel–lo there," said a good-looking thirtyish man lounging against the door of the gym. "I didn't get to meet you earlier. I'm Jerry Rawley."

Uh-oh. The gym teacher Mrs. Leeper warned her about. He didn't look too dangerous with his white Central Middle School polo and the waist of his burgundy polyester shorts pulled halfway to his armpits.

She extended her hand. "Hi. I'm Sunni Vanderclef."

He took her hand and shook it but didn't release it. "You certainly are. I can't tell you what a welcome addition you are to the Central faculty."

"Thank you." She maintained her smile while tugging at her hand.

He wasn't letting go. "I know it's tough starting new at school. I'd like to offer my services to help you get settled in."

He loosened his grip slightly to step closer, and Sunni seized the opportunity to snatch her hand away. She locked her hands behind her back. "That's so sweet of you, but Jennifer is showing me around."

He took another step toward her and lowered his voice suggestively. "Then we'll have to come up with another way to get to know each other better."

Sunni didn't think he was talking about school tours anymore. "Uh. . .I'll think about it," Sunni said as she inched back in retreat.

She ran into something solid, something too warm to be a wall. With a sinking feeling, she slowly turned around. "Hello, Mr. Harris. Coach Rawley was just offering me. . .a tour."

"I'll bet." He looked past her to the coach. "Jerry, I need that count on orange cones before two o'clock."

"Right. I'm on it." Jerry winked at Sunni and disappeared through the gym door.

Sunni watched him go. "Mrs. Leeper was right. That guy's an animal."

"It doesn't take much to set Jerry off. I'm sure your. . .uh"—he waved a careless hand in her direction—"outfit was more than he could resist."

She self-consciously smoothed her hands over the form-fitting slacks. "This outfit is stylish."

He shrugged. "Whatever you say. My professional advice to you is to tone down the stylish. Unless you like guys like Jerry hitting on you."

Though she knew he was right and that she wouldn't wear the slacks again, she had no intention of admitting it. "Thanks for the tip." Sunni turned to go.

"I'd like to talk to you, if you have a minute."

No way was she powwowing with the Grinch. "Sorry, I don't. I'm trying to decorate my classroom."

"Take a break," he commanded in a deceptively mild tone.

"Good idea."

She couldn't say she was happy to have run into Mr. Harris, but his appearance was a blessing in one regard. She'd never have found her way through the maze of halls to the front door without his leading the way. Too bad he was such a grouch. He was very good-looking.

She followed him past Mrs. Leeper and into his office. Once inside, he closed the door.

"Where were you this morning?"

Sunni didn't think she would ever get used to his abrupt style. "I assume you're asking me why I was a little late."

"Very astute. The meeting began at ten. You didn't stroll in until almost eleven."

She couldn't imagine why he was making such a big deal about such a tiny infraction. She'd been a lot later for much more important things than a silly teachers' meeting. "I had a previous commitment."

"Let me guess. Brunch with the garden club?"

His snippy remark goaded her into revealing more truth than was prudent. "No. An elevator sale at Sole Mates."

His brows shot sky-high. "You missed my meeting to buy an elevator?"

She was glad his door was closed so Mrs. Leeper couldn't hear him shout. She lowered her voice, hoping he'd be civilized enough to follow suit. "No, I didn't buy an elevator. I went to an elevator sale."

His handsome face turned an alarming shade of red.

She hurried on to explain. "An elevator sale means that the percentage off goes down every hour. When the store opened at ten, all the shoes were fifty percent off. At eleven, they were forty percent off, at noon—"

"—thirty percent off. I get it."

She didn't think he'd look so angry if he truly got it. "I didn't know what time the meeting would be over, and

I certainly didn't want to roll into the store at noon to shop picked-over inventory at inflated prices." Inspiration struck her. "If I'm going to be an effective home ec teacher, it's important that I practice what I preach. I was economizing."

"You walked into my meeting an hour late because you were buying a pair of shoes?"

"Three pairs actually. And when you multiply the fifty percent savings times three, you realize how smart it was of me to go early."

He moved across the room, placing his desk between them. Sunni had the funniest feeling he was separating himself for her well-being. "May I give you another professional tip?"

She was glad his tone of voice sounded reasonable. "Certainly."

"Don't be late for my meetings ever again. Not one minute. Ever. Do you understand?"

His tone might be reasonable, but his dark eyes glowed like a madman's. A homicidal madman. She nodded. "I understand."

"Good. That's all."

She turned to leave. She had her hand on the doorknob when he said, "Did you happen to pick up a pair of sensible flat shoes at the sale today?"

She recoiled in horror. "No!"

"Might I suggest you find another shoe sale between now and Monday and buy yourself a pair for teaching? You won't last two hours standing in front of a class in ice-pick heels."

She lifted her brows. "Is that another professional tip, Mr. Harris?"

He nodded. "Yes, I believe it is."

"Then I'll consider it."

Mrs. Leeper stopped Sunni as she stomped out of Mr. Harris's office. "There you are. I wanted to give you a copy of Kristen's lesson plans. You don't have to use them, of course, but they might come in handy until you settle in."

Sunni accepted them gratefully. "Thank you, Mrs. Leeper."

"It's Mr. Harris you ought to be thanking. It was his idea."

Sunni smiled. *Thank Mr. Harris?* Over her dead body.

three

Sunni stumbled into her kitchen and flicked on the coffee-maker. She couldn't remember the last time she'd been up at five thirty in the morning. Probably never. She yawned. She knew she needed to hurry if she was going to make it to the school by seven, but she wasn't going anywhere until she'd had a cup or two of strong coffee.

She picked up the book of lesson plans she'd left on the table last night. She'd intended to study it after dinner, but when her best friend dropped by to invite her to a party, the lesson plans had been forgotten. *Oh well*, she thought as she thumbed through the thick three-ring binder, *I'll look it over tonight*. It wasn't as if anybody taught anything on the first day of class anyway.

She lingered at the table for two cups of coffee, hoping the caffeine would jolt her awake. Still sleepy, she carried a third cup back to her bedroom to drink while she dressed.

At seven fifteen, Sunni strode through the front doors of Central Middle School, an Italian leather briefcase in one hand and a travel mug of coffee in the other. She ducked her head and hurried past the front office in case Mr. Harris was watching to see if she'd made it in on time.

Though school didn't start until eight, lots of kids were already in the halls. She hadn't realized junior-high students were so big. Most of the kids she passed towered over her, and she was wearing three-inch heels.

Junior-high kids weren't cute and cuddly the way she remembered her kindergartners to be. In fact, with their spiked hair, black T-shirts with band logos, and baggy jeans, they were downright intimidating.

The lights were already on in the home ec room. Sunni walked in, glad to see she was alone. She needed time to collect her thoughts and work up her courage before the students descended on her.

She laid her briefcase and mug on top of her desk and rubbed her sweaty palms together. Suddenly she was really scared. She didn't have any idea what she was doing. She'd taken the job to prove to Mason that she wasn't playing her life away, that she had purpose. The dramatic gesture seemed like a good way to make her point. Sure, she'd prayed about it, but she never dreamed she'd actually be standing in front of a class.

A half-dozen, official-looking memos and a computer roster for each of her classes were stacked on her chair. She picked them up, hoping they contained tips on how she was to proceed.

The first sheet of paper was a reminder to look for dress code infractions and send all violators to the office. She crumpled it up and threw it away. Unless someone strolled in barefoot and buck naked, she wasn't likely to recognize a dress code violation. She hadn't been paying attention when Mr. Harris reviewed the dress code on Saturday.

The second memo listed lunchroom policies and prices. Since it had TEACHERS: READ THIS TO YOUR HOMEROOM across the top, Sunni thought it was important enough to save.

The third and fourth sheets, also titled READ THIS TO YOUR HOMEROOM, outlined school guidelines for class times, behavior on campus, and dismissal procedures. She supposed she ought to read them, as well.

The last two sheets didn't have caps in the memo heading, so she wadded them up and added them to the trash. She had enough rules to burden the kids with on the first day. No point in overloading them.

She flipped through the rosters. She had six classes every day. *Six times twenty-four.* She had almost a hundred and fifty students!

She finished off her steaming coffee in one scalding gulp.

The classroom filled quickly. Finally reunited with other classmates after summer vacation, the students talked and laughed until the room was buzzing. When the noise level escalated to a roar, Sunni, who'd been standing at her desk smiling and nodding at each newcomer, knew she had to act.

"Good morning," she said, moving to the front of the room.

Nobody but the kids in the front row appeared to hear her, and they didn't care enough to interrupt their conversations.

She tried again. *Louder.* "Good morning. Let's get started."

Still no change.

Sunni walked to her desk, picked up her now empty aluminum travel mug and banged it on the desk. *Hard.* The loud clangs shocked everyone, not the least of them Sunni.

"Oh!" she said, wincing at the noise. "Good morning. Since we're all here, I suppose we ought to get started."

She moved back to the center front of the room and tried not to panic as twenty-four pairs of eyes homed in on her.

She barely resisted wringing her hands. "I'm Miss Vanderclef. I'm the new home ec teacher."

"Where's Miss Hobart?"

How should she know? And who was Miss Hobart? It dawned on Sunni that Miss Hobart was the wounded home ec teacher. "Would that be Kristen?" she asked to be sure.

The class giggled. *Interesting.* The fact that adults had first names must be funny to young teens.

Sunni took the giggles for affirmation. "Miss Hobart had an accident. She'll be fine, but she needs several months to recuperate."

"You don't look much like a teacher."

From what she'd seen of teachers, Sunni took that as a compliment. "Thanks."

They giggled again.

She picked up the memos she'd found on her chair and read them to the class. That took five minutes. *Now what?* "What do you usually do in homeroom?" she asked.

"On the first day of school, we get our locker assignments."

Yikes! Sunni didn't recall seeing locker assignments in the stack of papers.

"They're probably on the homeroom class list," some helpful soul prompted.

Sunni scanned the computer printout. Sure enough, locker numbers and combinations were printed beside each name. "Okay, let me call out your name, locker number, and combination."

The room erupted into cries of concern and outrage.

"You can't do that. Combinations are secret."

"Good point," Sunni admitted. "I'll come around to each desk. You give me your name, and I'll give you your locker number and combination."

"You're supposed to let us go try them out. To be sure we can get them open," someone suggested.

Made sense. "Fine. After I give you the information, step out into the hall and check to be sure you can open the locker."

Sunni took a pack of sticky notes from the top drawer and walked over to the kid in the front. "Hi. Who are you?"

"Robert Callahan."

Sunni scanned the roster, put a check beside Robert's name, and in her very best penmanship wrote out his locker assignment and combination on a pink sticky note. She handed it to him. "Go try this out."

Sunni continued around the room, passing out assignments. Odd that the first students hadn't returned yet from experimenting with their locks. By the time she'd finished with the last student, her classroom was empty. Evidently it took awhile to practice combinations.

She was halfway to the door to find out where they'd gone when an ear-piercing buzzer went off somewhere overhead, frightening a full year off Sunni's life. At the sound, the halls exploded into activity. Sunni watched wide-eyed as a sea of giggling, talking teenagers swarmed through the halls in a wave of denim.

Oh no! That buzzer must have signaled the end of homeroom. She hadn't even told her class good-bye.

A fresh batch of students poured in through her open door. By the time a second buzzer blared, all the desks were taken.

Sunni was struck with inspiration. She picked up a nice new piece of chalk from the tray and wrote her name, Miss Vanderclef, neatly on the board. She made a mental note that she'd have to practice writing without making that terrible screeching sound.

When she finished, she turned to face the class. "Good morning. I'm Miss Vanderclef. I'm your home ec teacher."

"Where's Miss Hobart?"

This time she was prepared. Sunni repeated the information about Kristen's accident and the assurance that Miss Hobart was resting comfortably.

"I only signed up for this class because of Miss Hobart," somebody called from the back of the room.

Just what every insecure new teacher wanted to hear. "I hope you'll enjoy my class," Sunni said.

"Are these assigned seats, or are you going to put us in alphabetical order to call roll?"

Roll! She'd been so wrapped up in lockers, she'd forgotten to take roll in homeroom. She hated to think what Mr. Harris would say if he heard about that.

"Alphabetical order," Sunni said after a moment's consideration.

The class groaned. Evidently alphabetical order wasn't a popular decision. Sunni was torn between changing her mind so the kids would like her and sticking with her original idea so the kids wouldn't think she was wishy-washy. Since they'd already begun climbing out of their seats, she may as well alphabetize them.

She picked up the roster. "Ricardo Acquillar, first row right."

The class snickered.

"What?" Sunni asked. "Did I mispronounce it?"

It took three minutes and a lot more snickering before she could say the young man's name to his satisfaction. She wrote the phonetic pronunciation in the margin of the roll so she wouldn't make that mistake again.

"Behind Ricardo, I want Lauren Bascom."

It took the entire class period to alphabetize twenty-four

students. She'd had to stop in the middle of the process to listen to the announcements blaring over the intercom.

The buzzer rang before she could swing up on her stool and tell them what they'd be studying over the year. Since she wasn't exactly sure what they'd be studying, she considered the buzzer fortuitous.

The first-period class filed out as the second-period class filed in. Having learned by her previous mistakes, she made seat assignments as they walked in. She'd successfully taken roll and fielded questions about the absent Miss Hobart and still had twenty-five minutes left in the class period.

She would have been on cloud nine if it weren't for the fact she needed to use the rest room. All that coffee had come back to haunt her.

What to do? Her limited experience told her there wasn't enough time to go anywhere between class periods. Even if she knew where the teachers' lounge was located, she didn't think she could travel the crowded halls to the rest room and back in the time allotted to change classes.

According to her rosters, she didn't have a free class period until one forty-five. No way could she wait until then. If she read the schedule correctly, she had lunch at eleven fifty-one, but even that was too long a wait for a woman who'd downed four cups of coffee by eight o'clock.

Forget dress codes and district policies—*this* was the sort of situation Mr. Harris should be covering in his meetings.

With twenty-five minutes until the buzzer, now seemed as good a time as any. But what did she do with the class? Sunni's gaze came to rest on the cardboard box of supplies she'd used as a student teacher. *Bingo.*

She picked up the box and carried it to the rows of desks. She counted out six boxes of crayons or markers and placed them on the front desk of each row. "Take one and pass the rest back."

Even something as simple as taking a box and passing the rest seemed to stir up a discussion. Once the crayons were distributed, she handed out a sheet of construction paper to each student.

"What I'd like each of you to do is create a name tag to hang on the front of your desk." *Hmm.* Writing their names wouldn't give her enough time to find the rest room and make it back. "In addition to writing your name, I'd like you to decorate the tag in a way that illustrates your personality."

No sooner were the words out of her mouth than she was bombarded with questions.

"I don't understand."

"Can you repeat the instructions?"

"Do we get a grade on this?"

Sunni repeated the instructions slowly. "While you are working, I'm going to step out for just a moment. I want you all to be very quiet." Their smiles were so angelic she should have known to expect trouble.

She trotted down the empty halls as fast as she could on three-inch heels. She never did find the teachers' lounge, but there was a girls' room at the end of C Hall.

Sunni felt in harmony with the world as she walked back to her room less than five minutes later. She was proud to note that no noise drifted out of her classroom into the hall. *Bless their little hearts.*

She entered her room. "Thank you so much for being so qui—oh! Mr. Harris."

❧

If he hadn't been so angry, he'd probably have found her

shocked expression amusing. As it was, he couldn't muster up the smallest smile for Ms. Vanderclef, who stood in the doorway with her lips frozen in a perfect O and the blood draining from her face.

What was she thinking, walking out on her class like that?

He unfolded himself from her chair. "I was down at the far end of the hall when I heard what sounded like a party. A very loud party. I traced the noise to your classroom."

Sunni scowled at the now subdued students. "I'm so sorry. I asked them to be quiet. They assured me they would."

"It seems they forgot." He folded his arms across his chest and gave her a pointed look. "They didn't know where you were."

"They must be extremely forgetful. I know I told them I was going to slip out for a minute or two."

She was evading his implied question. She had no intention of telling him where she'd been. She honestly believed she could disappear with no explanation. He'd see about that.

"I'll leave you to your class," Ethan said. "I know you have important material to cover with them before the bell rings."

"Thank you, Mr. Harris." Sunni flashed him a self-satisfied smile. Her smug expression said it all. She was brushing him off.

He strode from her classroom. How dare she defy him? He was the principal. It was his right—his responsibility—to know where his teachers were and who was watching each class.

He couldn't very well demand an explanation from her in front of the students. A wise man knew to handle his problems discreetly. But a wise man also knew he had to confront problems head-on before they became a bigger problem.

Ethan was so wrapped up in the big problem, aka Sunni Vanderclef, that he hardly noticed Coach Rawley standing in the doorway of the gym, grinning like an idiot.

"Hello, Ethan," Coach Rawley said with a nod.

"How's it going, Jerry?" Ethan didn't stop to chat as a new thought had occurred to him. Five minutes was plenty of time for an assignation with a woman-crazy PE coach. It seemed suspicious that both Ms. Vanderclef and Jerry were wearing similar grins. And, come to think of it, he hadn't seen Jerry anywhere when he'd gone to investigate the noise emanating from the home ec room.

Ethan's temper boiled hotter. To abandon her class was bad enough, but to use valuable class time for her personal flirtations was unacceptable.

He stewed over the increasingly lurid scenario all day. At two forty-five, he stepped out of his office. "Mrs. Leeper, would you please call down to Ms. Vanderclef's room and tell her I'd like to see her in my office after dismissal?"

Mrs. Leeper picked up on his grim tone. "Is there a problem?"

He was tempted to say Ms. Vanderclef was a problem. "No. I just want to see how her first day went."

Mrs. Leeper flashed him a look of admiration. "You are such a thoughtful man."

"Thank you. I hope Ms. Vanderclef sees it that way."

Mrs. Leeper flipped on the intercom for the home ec room. "Ms. Vanderclef?"

On the other end, Sunni shrieked at the loud, surprise interruption. "Hello? Yes?"

"I'm sorry to bother you, but Mr. Harris has asked me to call. He'd like to see you in his office after dismissal."

The students singsonged a loud *uh-oh* before Sunni answered. "Thank you, Mrs. Leeper. I'll be there."

❧

Ethan positioned himself behind his desk for Ms. Vanderclef's appointment. That way, if the urge to strangle her became too strong, he could rethink his actions in the time it took to get around the desk. He prayed for patience, reminding God that hiring Sunni was His idea, but was in no mood to wait for an answer.

Ms. Vanderclef arrived with a smile. "You wanted to see me?"

Ethan allowed himself a moment to see her through Jerry's eyes. It was obvious why someone who didn't realize she was nothing but a spoiled rich girl would fall for her. Sunni Vanderclef was beautiful. Hers was a classic beauty with elegant features and an aristocratic bone structure. Her blue eyes sparkled, and her lips were turned up in a smile. Her thick shoulder-length blond hair tempted his fingers to reach out and muss it. Her tailored powder blue suit draped an attractive figure.

Combine beauty with an innate cheerfulness, and Ms. Vanderclef added up to one appealing female.

A female who was driving him crazy.

His long silent perusal must have unnerved her. She dropped her gaze to her hands clasped in front of her. "If this is about this morning, I'm sorry."

"Where were you?"

Her head shot up. "Excuse me?"

"I asked you where you were when I found your class unsupervised."

She looked distinctly uncomfortable. "Oh. Personal business."

Aha. Just as he suspected. She was meeting Coach Rawley

on the sly. "Personal business that couldn't wait?"

"Yeah," she said with a self-conscious grin. "I was pretty desperate."

Ethan shot to his feet with the intention of going over the top of the desk. "Desperate?" he roared. "Desperate?"

She retreated a step. "I had to use the rest room."

Her softly spoken words penetrated the red haze of his brain. He froze. "What?"

"I said I had to use the rest room."

She hadn't been meeting Jerry. She had to use the rest room. Such an obvious explanation. Why hadn't he thought of it? It was her fault. She was messing with his mind.

Boy, did he feel like an idiot. Talk about overreacting. Since he'd already dug himself in pretty deep with the Gestapo-like interrogation, he couldn't very well drop the whole thing and send her away. He might be losing his mind, but he didn't want the fact to become public knowledge.

He reseated himself and folded his hands on the desk. He spoke in his best so-you've-been-sent-to-the-principal voice. "You went to the rest room during class time?"

His earlier explosion seemed to have set her off. "Do you have a better suggestion?" she snapped.

"Teachers use their free period to take care of personal matters."

"My free period, if you can call wading through stacks of useless memos 'free time,' wasn't until one forty-five."

"And your point is?"

She slapped her perfectly manicured hands on her waist. "My point is, I drank four cups of coffee before eight o'clock. I'm only five feet three. Short people don't come with forty-ounce bladders."

Forty-ounce bladders? It was all Ethan could do not to laugh. He had to chew the insides of his mouth and stare at his folded hands a full twenty seconds to control himself. When he lifted his eyes to hers, he trained his mouth in a stern line. "May I offer you a word of advice?"

"I'd be disappointed if you didn't."

"Don't drink four cups of coffee before school."

He saw her clench her hands into fists and imagined she'd like to use them on him. Her voice was tight and controlled. "Thank you, Mr. Harris. I'll try to remember that."

four

Sunni buried her face in her brown paper grocery sack as she sped past Mr. Harris's office at seven fourteen on Tuesday morning. She'd messed up big yesterday. She'd have to work extra hard to toe the line if she was going to keep her job. She'd hardly impress Mason with her new career if she worked less than a week.

She tossed her purse under her desk in the home ec room, then continued on to the kitchens. She stopped at each one and placed a bag of chocolate chips on the counter and two pounds of butter and a dozen eggs in each refrigerator.

Busy kids were happy kids. Her students were going to be busy today baking chocolate chip cookies.

When she'd distributed the supplies, she carried the grocery bag with the other thirty bags of chocolate chips back to her desk and slid it underneath. She didn't want anybody to spot the extras and walk off with them. She had five more classes to supply.

Chocolate chip cookies weren't in the lesson plans. She'd flipped through the home ec lesson plan binder while stopped at a red light on her way home from school yesterday and discovered the first two weeks were dedicated to a study of cooking and nutrition basics. The information couldn't hold her attention until the light turned green; how could she expect active teenagers to be interested in such dull stuff?

Baking cookies would be something everyone could enjoy.

She thought her homeroom went nicely. She arranged them in alphabetical order and made a neat check in the box beside each name on the roll to indicate they were present. Like yesterday, she had no absentees, so she didn't have to send any special slips down to the attendance office. When the buzzer sounded overhead, Sunni sent them off with a smile.

So far, so good.

"Good morning," she said to her first-period class after they'd settled into their seats. "I have a surprise planned for you today. We're going to bake chocolate chip cookies."

The class burst into excited chatter, and Sunni knew she'd been smart to go with her instincts and forgo two long boring weeks of basics.

"I'm going to separate you into groups and assign each group to a kitchen." She had to talk louder to be heard over the noise. "To save time, I want the front row to go to kitchen one, the second row to go to kitchen two, the third row to go to kitchen three, and so on."

One kid in the back row shot his hand in the air. "So where do I go?"

Obviously not a rocket scientist. "You're in the sixth row," Sunni explained. "That means you will go to kitchen six."

Chaos reigned. Such simple instructions generated confusion and discussion. Sunni moved to the center of the room and clapped her hands to get attention.

"Quiet, please. We don't have time to waste. Look around. There should be four students in each kitchen."

Several students who'd reassigned themselves to a kitchen with a friend shuffled back to their original kitchen assignment.

"I want one person in each group of four to be the team leader today. Rather than wasting time with a vote, I want the person who sits at the right end of the row to be team leader."

She should have expected the ensuing confusion about whose right she was talking about. Precious time ticked by while she went from kitchen to kitchen to appoint leaders.

She moved back to the center of the room. "Our team leaders will be in charge of reading the recipes for the group."

"I didn't get one!"

Sunni raised a hand for silence. "Everyone got one. The recipes we will be using are found on the side of the chocolate chip packages. Team leaders will delegate jobs within the teams. I want each person to have at least one task. Don't worry if you don't get to do everything today. We'll have plenty of opportunities for cooking over the coming year."

Whether or not the seventh graders learned anything in home ec class that day, Sunni learned plenty.

She learned that unless you watched them like a hawk, seventh-grade boys will eat all the chocolate chips before the dough is mixed.

She learned that accurate measurements were relative and that breaking eggs is much more difficult than it looks.

Finally she learned that no one in their right mind would attempt to supervise six kitchens of novice cooks. If she ever decided to have her classes bake cookies again, it would be the slice-and-bake kind from the grocery store.

"Miss Vanderclef? I got eggshell in the cookie dough."

"That's okay," Sunni said. "I'll fish it out."

"You can't. Eileen already stirred it in."

Sunni patted the tearful would-be chef on the shoulder.

"Don't worry. A little shell won't hurt."

"It's more than just a little." She sniffled again as she held up the two halves of the eggshell with a large chunk missing from the break line.

Sunni shook her head. "Just stir the batter more. It'll break up the shell fragments so small that nobody will notice them." She made a mental note not to sample any of the cookies from kitchen five.

In spite of minor problems in every kitchen, the first batches finally went into the ovens. For kitchen two, it would be the first and only batch because they had eaten the rest of the dough.

While the cookies baked, Sunni had each group wash out their mixing bowls and utensils and put away leftover ingredients. In ten minutes, the cookies came out of the ovens fragrant and golden brown. The finished cookies were transferred to platters, and the rest of the dough was spooned into uniform globs onto the cookie sheets.

Sunni looked at the clock. Seven minutes till the dismissal buzzer. She scooted around to each kitchen and cranked up the ovens to 475 degrees to shave off a little baking time.

She'd turned up the last oven when a scuffle in kitchen five demanded her attention.

"What's the trouble?" she asked the two combatants.

"She bumped my arm and made some of the cookie dough slide off into the bottom of the oven."

"It was my turn to put in the cookie sheet. It's not fair that he got to put in both batches."

Sunni couldn't imagine what was so all-fired exciting about placing a cookie sheet in the oven. She raised her hand for silence. "That's enough. Next time we bake, it'll be your turn to put in the cookies. Right now, I want you to take a couple of cookies, put them on a napkin, and eat them at your desk while we wait for this batch to bake."

The kitchens were straightened up by the time the second batch finished. The cookies were a bit dark, probably from being baked at too high a temperature, but the kids didn't seem to mind.

When the buzzer sounded for dismissal, each proud student carried a small aluminum packet of homemade cookies. Sunni stood in the doorway to say good-bye and share a word of praise. As the last student filed out, she collapsed against the door and wondered how she'd manage five more frantic cooking sessions.

Her second-period students arrived in a rambunctious wave. Word traveled fast in the middle school, and they were ecstatic about the prospect of baking and eating cookies in class.

After they were seated, Sunni took the roll.

"Miss Vanderclef?" The girl with the glasses in the second row raised her hand. "I smell something burning."

Sunni smelled it, too. She figured it was the residual smell from the slightly burned batch of cookies from first period. "It's the ovens," she said. "We turned them up extra high last period."

Sunni didn't have time to trot back there right now, so she made a mental note to turn down the ovens to 350 degrees while the kids mixed up the dough.

The smell didn't dissipate. If anything, the burning smell grew stronger during her instructions and team assignments. It couldn't be anything in her room. The ovens were empty.

A loud clanging bell rang out as Sunni opened her mouth to send each team to their kitchens.

"What does that mean?" she asked the class.

"Fire drill."

You didn't need to be a home ec major to know how to conduct a fire drill. With an efficiency she didn't know she possessed, Sunni lined up her suddenly subdued students and marched them out the nearest exit. She led her class into the freshly mowed soccer field where the other teachers were standing with their classes. The home ec class fell in beside Jennifer Stanton's science class.

Sunni was glad to see her friend. "Do you usually have a fire drill on the second day of school?"

Jennifer shook her head. "Never, that I can remember. We usually have one within the first month, but in the past, Mr. Harris has given us a heads-up that it's coming."

Sunni thought about the mysterious burning smell in her classroom. "It *is* a drill, isn't it? I mean, you don't think something like an overheated oven could set off the alarms, do you?"

"Sure, it's a drill. Maybe the district wanted to see how we handled an unannounced drill."

The bright morning sunshine and fresh air had a reviving effect on her unusually cooperative class, and in minutes, they reverted to their original noisy, wiggly selves. Sunni excused herself to see about a pair of obnoxious boys who were circling one another in a mock fistfight. At the sight of the pair of fire trucks coming up the road, sirens wailing, the class once again fell silent. Dread made Sunni's limbs wobbly as she scrambled to Jennifer's side. "Do they usually dispatch fire trucks to a drill?"

Puzzled, Jennifer shook her head. "Not that I'm aware of."

Sunni couldn't shake the sick feeling in the pit of her

stomach that the arrival of the fire trucks and the burning smell in her classroom were somehow related. The feeling intensified as she saw Mr. Harris, more grim-faced than usual, set out across the field with something in his hands and a fully uniformed fireman in tow. She knew instinctively that he was headed her way.

She could run.

With a thirty-second head start, she could be in her car and out of the parking lot. If only she had her car keys.

Mr. Harris and the fireman were closing in.

If she was going to escape, now was the time. The truth was, she could run, but she couldn't hide. She hadn't known him long, but she was certain Mr. Harris would track her to the ends of the earth.

Running wasn't that great of an option anyway. She'd look foolish, he'd probably catch her, and even if she managed to escape, she'd ruin her lovely new tan suede shoes with grass stains.

He was close enough for her to see his face. It was bright sunburn red, whether from exertion or provocation she couldn't say, and his eyes glittered with an otherworldly light.

Sunni swallowed hard. She should have run.

He stopped ten feet from where she quavered in her stilettos. "Ms. Vanderclef. May I have a word with you?" he said in a voice weighted with doom.

The whispers behind her sounded like a thousand buzzing locusts.

She stepped forward. "Yes, Mr. Harris?"

"Our friends from the fire department received an alarm from the school. The sensors detected smoke in the home ec room."

"Funny you should mention it. I thought I smelled something burning in the classroom, but that's impossible. The ovens were hot, but empty."

The fireman shifted his helmet back to see her better. "Actually, ma'am, we found something burning in one of the ovens. It's difficult to identify, but it appears to be some food substance that caught fire in the extreme heat."

Mr. Harris extended his hand. A small black lump sat in the middle of a blue calico pot holder. "Any ideas?"

It smelled awful. Sunni inched closer, her hand over her nose, and examined the charred remains.

She shook her head. "I can't imagine what it could be—wait." A thin white sliver protruded from the base of the black glob. *Eggshell!*

Sunni beamed into the perspiring face of the fireman. "I bet you found this in kitchen five, the back right unit."

"That's right."

"It's cookie dough," she announced with the aplomb of Sherlock Holmes when he hit upon the solution to a great mystery. "The kids accidentally dropped a cookie when they were sliding in the cookie sheet. In the confusion of one class leaving and another arriving, I forgot all about it. Sorry." She flashed them both a sheepish grin and shrugged.

Mr. Harris didn't look as if he were ready to forgive and forget. "Ms. Vanderclef, your forgetfulness cost the taxpayers considerable expense. The city had to dispatch trucks and men to investigate. That doesn't take into account the forty-five minutes of class time our students have wasted standing out here."

She'd already apologized. She didn't know what else he wanted from her. "I'm sorry about the lost class time, although we couldn't have picked a prettier day to stand around outside. The kids seem to be enjoying the fresh air."

She turned to the fireman and smiled. "Your response time is impressive. It's good to know that help is on its way so quickly."

Mr. Harris rolled his eyes. "Captain Denby, I'm sure you have something to say to Ms. Vanderclef. I have to get these kids back inside."

♠

Mrs. Leeper was already at her desk by the time Ethan had rounded up all the classes and sent them back into the building. She looked up and smiled as he entered the office. "Mr. Harris, you have a call on line two. Kristen Hobart calling for you."

"Thanks." He closed the door to his office and sat behind the desk. He picked up the receiver and punched line two. "Hi, Kristen. How are you feeling?"

"Rotten. Any illusions I had about the glamour of staying in a hospital have been shattered. This place is horrible. Oh, thanks for the flowers. They are the only bright spot within these four walls."

"I don't want to make it too pleasant. We want you back as soon as possible."

"How's it going, Ethan? Have you found someone to take my classes?"

"What I found is a walking disaster. A woman came in the day of your accident looking for a job. Her credentials weren't bad, and her timing was impeccable so I hired her. I haven't had a moment's peace since she arrived."

"School's been in session less than two days. I don't see how she could have messed up in such a short time."

Ethan snorted. "She's amazing. She's been an hour late for a mandatory meeting, walked out in the middle of a class, and the fire trucks are just now pulling away."

"Fire trucks?"

"It's too painful to go into detail. Suffice it to say, you have to get the doctor to fit you in a walking body cast. We need you back."

Kristen laughed. "Don't make me laugh. It hurts."

"Does it help to know I'm doing my fair share of suffering since you've been gone?" Ethan asked.

"It's flattering to be missed, but I hate to think you're miserable. Is she a first-time teacher?"

"Yeah."

"Then you don't need to worry. Give her a couple of days to get acclimated, and she'll be fine. I'm sure she lacks confidence."

"No," Ethan said. "I think it goes deeper than that. I think she lacks talent."

❧

As per Ethan's instructions, Mrs. Leeper called Sunni's classroom at two forty-five and asked her to come to Mr. Harris's office after school dismissal. He was seated behind his desk when she arrived.

"Hi, Mr. Harris. Mrs. Leeper told me you wanted to see me."

He didn't know how she managed to look so fresh and lovely at the end of the day. For some reason, it annoyed him. He sat back in his chair, propped his elbows on the desk, and steepled his fingers. "Yes. I want to know if you've been sent by some rival of mine to infiltrate my school and destroy it."

Her big blue eyes grew bigger. "Are you serious?"

"It sounds a bit far-fetched, but I can't think of another

explanation for how one woman can wreak so much havoc."

She looked guilty. "I guess I have hit a few rough patches since you hired me."

"It goes beyond rough patches. You're a menace."

Sunni frowned. "Menace seems a bit harsh. I was a little late for one meeting—"

"—an hour late for the only meeting we've had."

"And I took care of a personal matter during class time—"

"—leaving twenty-four seventh graders unsupervised."

"And burned up one small cookie—"

"—causing the entire school to be evacuated while the fire department searched for the source of the fire."

"Okay," she conceded. "That was pretty awful. But it was a mistake. Everybody is entitled to a mistake or two as they settle in to a new job."

"Not if their mistakes jeopardize the operations of the school. I don't think you realize it, but Central Middle School is a very special school. With hard work and dedication, we've built the reputation of being the best. We are in the running to be designated as a Blue Ribbon school again this year, and I don't want anything or anybody to mess it up."

"I can appreciate your concern, and I want you to know I'll do everything in my power to see that we remain a Blue Ribbon school."

He could see she meant it. Still, he felt that after all the trouble she'd caused he was letting her off too easy. Somebody ought to scorch her ears with a lecture about excellence and taking responsibility. She needed to know her performance was substandard and her job was on the line.

But it was tough to think substandard when she was standing there, beautiful and brave, maintaining her considerable poise even as he could see the beginning of tears pool in her eyes.

No, he couldn't deliver the well-deserved lecture when she looked like that. If anything good came out of today's fiasco with the fire department, it was that Captain Denby had a reputation as a real hardnose. He wouldn't have any problem saying what needed to be said.

"So what did Captain Denby have to say?"

"Captain Denby? Oh, the nice fireman who walked me back to class." She frowned. "Are you sure you want to know?"

He was practically rubbing his hands together in anticipation. "Absolutely."

She shrugged. "He laughed at what a terrible cook I am and said I'd probably starve if somebody didn't step in. Then he asked me out for dinner Friday night."

five

Sunni sleepwalked into Central Middle School at five minutes past seven. She was too tired to care if Mr. Harris saw her come in late, though she personally maintained that arriving within five minutes of the established start time qualified as being early.

Her briefcase banged heavily against her leg as she headed for her classroom. It was filled with the handouts she'd created the night before. The little incident with the fire department yesterday convinced her that she and the class could use a dose of basic training before she unleashed them on the kitchens.

To that end, she'd stayed up most of the night reading through Miss Hobart's lesson plans. Sunni didn't think she wanted to use them exactly as written, so she adapted the curriculum into a lesson plan she found more appealing. From the new plans, she drew up a calendar of daily topics she would cover from now to the end of the first semester and printed off a copy to distribute to each student. She didn't believe they'd look at the calendar, but it seemed like a teacher thing to do.

Sunni was feeling quite "teachery" this morning. She'd read up on today's topic and even made notes to lecture from. The realization she was prepared sent a nice warm glow through her.

Not only did she feel like a teacher, but also this morning, she looked the part. Her sleeveless hot pink linen dress and matching jacket were bright and cheerful and even professional looking. After much internal debate, she left off the single strand of pearls. She was going for teacher, not Mrs. Cleaver. She'd slept through her alarm, so she'd had to scoop her hair into an upswept style that gave her a prim, competent look. She was sure even Mr. Harris would think she was every inch the teacher today.

She didn't have to wait long to find out. The principal arrived unexpectedly with her first-class period. The kids were delighted when he pulled an empty chair to the back of the room and sat with the obvious intention of staying.

Sunni felt sick. Three hours of sleep seemed inadequate fortification to be lecturing under his dark-eyed scrutiny.

"Good morning," she said after the buzzer sounded. "It's nice to see all your smiling faces. And as an extra bonus, we have Mr. Harris with us today." She aimed a smile at him. "Welcome."

The kids turned in their desks to greet him. For some unknown reason, they seemed to like their principal. He must possess some well-hidden good quality Sunni had yet to see.

"Was there something you wanted to share with us this morning?" she asked him.

"No. I'm just here to observe."

That sounded ominous.

"I don't want to interrupt anything," he continued. "Pretend I'm not here."

As if that will happen. He might be a thorn in her side, but he was a disturbingly attractive thorn. She thought if they'd met under different circumstances he'd be the type of man she'd like to know better. *Very different circumstances.*

Sunni grabbed the stack of calendars she'd printed off for

first period. She counted out six for each row, seven for the row Mr. Harris occupied. "If you'll go ahead and pass these back while I take the roll."

A young man with baggy shorts and a Curious George T-shirt appeared in her doorway.

"Can I help you?" Sunni asked.

"The lady in the office sent me," he said, advancing into the room to hand Sunni a sheet of paper. "I'm joining the class."

She read his name off the form. "That's wonderful, Jarred. Are you new to the school?"

"No, I've been here, but I used to be in band. I transferred out because I heard home ec was more fun."

Sunni shot a triumphant smile to Mr. Harris. "What a nice thing to say. I hope you'll enjoy it here."

"I'm sure I will. We never have fires in band."

Sunni kept the smile on her face as the class burst into laughter. She refused to look at Mr. Harris who was no doubt laughing at her, as well.

"You're lucky," Sunni said. "The custodian delivered an extra desk yesterday."

"If the demand for home ec gets too great, we'll have to open another section," Mr. Harris offered, barely suppressing his mirth.

Very funny. Sunni ignored him.

"Jarred, scoot that desk behind the last desk in row one. We'll decide later which kitchen to assign you to."

She picked up a copy of the calendar while Jarred moved his desk into place. "You all just received a class schedule for the current semester. If you'll look at it with me for a moment, I want to talk briefly about the things we'll be studying."

Sunni went over the information with the class. She was delighted that the kids seemed enthusiastic about the plans. Better, Mr. Harris wasn't wearing his usual Big Bad Principal expression. He was sitting forward in his seat, nodding and smiling as she spoke.

"Put those in your binder for reference," Sunni said as she finished. "It'll be a great way to keep up with what information will be on your tests."

While they rustled around putting the calendars away, Sunni dragged her stool to the front. She hadn't had an opportunity to use it yet. Sitting on a stool to lecture would cap off today's total teaching look.

She picked up her notes and walked to the stool trying to figure out the best way to mount it. The seat was taller than she remembered. She tried backing up to it and rising up on her tiptoes. No good. Even on tiptoes, she couldn't reach the seat.

By now, the class had put away their papers, and their full attention was focused on her.

"Today we'll start with an introduction to nutrition." Sunni backed up against the stool again, this time adding a little hop once she was on tiptoe. Her backside skimmed the seat of the stool. That was close. If she could get a little more lift, she'd be on it.

She raised up on tiptoe. "Nutrition by our definition is a study of food substances and their values to the human"—she hopped—"body."

The last word came out with a bit more force as she landed successfully on the seat with a *whoosh*.

She glanced up to see Mr. Harris silently applauding. She felt the heat rush down to the soles of her feet. *Does the man miss nothing?*

As she lectured, she realized that mounting the stool was only the beginning. After a bit of discreet experimentation, she discovered if she angled her body, turning her knees to the side wall of the classroom, and kept one hand pressed into her lap that she was able to maintain her modesty. Mr. Harris watched her every move.

Sunni came to a break in the lecture. "Does anyone have any questions?"

Several hands popped up. *Yikes!* She issued a silent prayer that she'd know the answers before calling on the first young man.

"I don't see why guys have to learn about calories."

Sunni relaxed. That wasn't too tough. "That's a reasonable question. Would anyone like to answer him before I do?"

Several girls raised their hands. "Eileen, tell us why you think men need to understand calories."

At that moment, an electronic version of the "Hallelujah Chorus" rang out. All talking ceased. Mr. Harris straightened, like a setter on point, trying to find the source. Cell phones were forbidden on campus.

Sunni knew by the distinctive ring that it was her phone. Why hadn't she remembered to switch if off when she entered the building?

She pretended she didn't hear the cheerful tune. She knew the phone would ring a couple of times; then her voice mail would pick it up, and the song would cease.

"Go ahead, Eileen," she prompted.

Eileen hesitated a second more, then said over the music, "Because if they don't understand calories, they'll get fat."

The chorus stopped. Sunni breathed a sigh of relief and a silent hallelujah of her own. "Thank you, Eileen. That's an excellent reason to understand calories. Does anyone else want to answer his question?"

Another tinkling round of the "Hallelujah Chorus" rent the air. *Oh no!* Whoever was calling wasn't satisfied to leave a message. The students darted glances back and forth, trying to discover the whereabouts of the contraband.

One helpful hand shot up. "Miss Vanderclef, I think the ringing is coming from under your desk."

Sunni went for a surprised look but suspected her smile was pained. "I think you're right."

"Maybe you should answer it. It might be important."

It was probably her hairdresser confirming her appointment. "No, I'm sure it's nothing. Let's ignore it. It'll stop in a moment."

Even as she spoke, it stopped. "There now, where were we? The importance of understanding calories."

When the phone started playing a third time, she knew she had to answer it. She slid off the stool. "Excuse me. This will only take a second."

She sat behind her desk and reached down to pull the singing phone from her purse. She put it to her ear, careful not to look at Mr. Harris who was surely apoplectic by now. "Hello?"

She kept her head bent so she was partially hidden by the desk. "Hi, Nicole," she whispered, aware that every pair of ears in the room was trained on her conversation. "Can I call you back later? I'm in the middle of teaching a class. . . . No, I'm not mad. I had to work on lesson plans. . . . Yes, I'm sure. Really. . . . Look, Nicole—I've really got to go. I'll call you later. Bye."

Sunni switched off the phone and slipped it back into her purse.

She wasn't surprised when Mrs. Leeper called down at two

forty-five to say Mr. Harris would like to see her in his office after school.

ja

"Hi, Mr. Harris. I suppose you asked for this meeting because you want to know why my cell phone went off during class."

Her direct approach surprised him. Some of the abruptness she'd accused him of must be wearing off on her. "Actually I know why it went off. You neglected to turn it off."

"You're right. I was so totally into nutrition that the phone slipped my mind."

"Are you interested in nutrition, Ms. Vanderclef?"

"I didn't think so. I mean, what's so great about the four basic food groups? But I guess I am. You wouldn't believe the amazing stuff I learned last night when I read the chapter in the textbook. I could hardly put the book down."

He smiled at her over steepled fingers. "Your enthusiasm showed."

"It did?" she asked.

He could tell she didn't know whether that was a good thing or a bad thing. Probably because he'd never said anything nice to her before.

He decided to help her out. He nodded. "When a teacher is excited about a topic, some of her enthusiasm is transferred to her students. Enthusiastic students learn better."

Sunni seemed to ponder what he'd said. "Are you saying I did something right?"

It was an effort to keep his expression solemn. "Yes, I am."

"Wow."

"But it doesn't do any good to have an enthusiastic class if the teacher is busy chatting on her phone when she should be teaching."

"I'm sure you're right."

"Always. That's why the district hired me."

"It must be nice to always be right." She turned to go. "Sorry about the phone. I won't let it happen again."

He hated to see her smile was gone. "Aren't you going to wait for my professional advice?"

"I didn't know you had any."

"A good principal is always brimming with professional advice."

Her smile was guarded. "Okay, go ahead."

"Turn the ringer off when you pull into the parking lot in the morning. Turn it back on when you get into your car in the afternoon. Think bumper to bumper."

&

Sunni ran into Jennifer, the science teacher, in the hall outside Mr. Harris's office.

Jennifer grinned. "Don't tell me you were back in there today?" she asked, jerking her shoulder toward his door.

Sunni nodded. "Yup. I'm three for three."

Jennifer fell into step alongside her. "I think you may be going for a record."

"Yeah."

Jennifer stopped. "What's the matter? You're not upset, are you? I was just teasing."

"No, I'm not upset." Sunni could feel tears burning at the back of her eyes.

"Come on—don't cry. Tell you what. I'm going to grab a couple of sodas from the teachers' lounge, and I'll meet you in the home ec room. We'll talk."

"Okay."

Jennifer must have run to be in Sunni's room so quickly.

She had two cans of diet soda in one hand and a huge bag of chips in the other. "I found the chips on the lunch table. I figured the person who left them there would want to share them with us."

Sunni grinned at the bald-faced piracy. "No doubt."

Jennifer pulled up a chair next to Sunni's desk. They popped the tops on their sodas and picnicked on sour cream-and-onion potato chips.

"So," Jennifer said after a few minutes of snacking, "tell me about it."

Sunni shrugged. "Not much to tell. Mr. Harris thinks I'm a menace."

Jennifer's red brows shot to her hairline. "He said that?"

"Exact words."

Jennifer frowned. "That doesn't sound like Ethan. He's usually such a nice guy."

"I must bring out a different side of his personality." Sunni took a swig of her soda. "What do you think I'm doing wrong?"

"What? Besides trying to burn down the school?"

Sunni winced.

Jennifer laughed and patted her on the back. "Don't take it to heart. The smoldering cookie dough was a fluke. It could happen to anyone."

"But it didn't. It happened to me. All the crazy things happen to me. Maybe Mr. Harris is right. I am a menace."

"Don't be so hard on yourself. I don't think Ethan meant it. It's just that you've got big shoes to fill."

"How's that?"

"You haven't heard about Kristen?"

"Kristen Hobart? Isn't she the teacher I'm replacing?"

"Yup."

"All the kids have asked about her. I get the impression she was a favorite. She was good, huh?"

Jennifer nodded. "The best. A real natural at teaching. And cooking. She used to cook gourmet stuff all the time and bring it to the teachers' lounge for us to sample."

Sunni was impressed. "Gourmet? Really?"

"Yeah. She used to come up with original recipes and enter them in contests. She's even had a recipe published in *Southern Living*. I think the clipping from the magazine is hanging on the wall in here."

Sunni pointed to the right wall. "It must be that laminated page with the spray-painted, Popsicle-stick frame. I thought about taking it down to hang a poster there, but I was afraid to move it. With those plastic flowers tucked in around it, it kind of looks like a shrine."

Jennifer squinted to see what Sunni was pointing at. "That's the one. Kristen is totally creative. She once made a scale model of the school for parents' night using empty milk cartons from the cafeteria."

"Okay, I'm going out on a limb here, but that sounds tacky to me."

Jennifer laughed. "I'm so glad to hear you say that. I thought it was horrible, but of course I didn't say so. Everybody acted as if it was the eighth wonder of the world."

"I didn't mean to sound critical," Sunni said. "Building with milk cartons takes ingenuity. I'm sure she's very talented."

"Very. Every year, she comes up with an amazing craft idea for the eighth-grade class fund-raiser. Last year, they made these plastic-bead cougars for the kids to hang on their backpacks. They netted four thousand dollars."

Sunni had seen the beaded creatures dangling from packs. She couldn't decide what was more amazing—coming up with the concept or paying money to own one. "Wow."

"Kristen was voted Teacher of the Year three years in a row. I guess this year will finally break her streak."

"I get the picture. Kristen is a paragon. No wonder Mr. Harris loves her."

Jennifer scooted her chair closer to Sunni's and lowered her voice. "You know, I think that's what Kristen is shooting for. She's trying to nab Ethan."

Sunni frowned. "Why?"

Jennifer laughed. "That's the disgruntled employee talking. Try to forget he's always yelling at you. Try to look at him simply as a man."

Sunni closed her eyes and conjured a picture of her boss in her mind. "Wow."

"Exactly. Ethan Harris is a prime specimen. He's very closemouthed about his private life, but I know he comes from a good family and he's a Christian. At thirty, he's the youngest principal in the district. And he's single. Good looks, good family, good job. What's not to love? If I weren't engaged, I'd make a play for him myself."

"Does Mr. Harris return Kristen's feelings?"

Jennifer shrugged. "I don't know. I know he likes her. But I've watched them together at school stuff, and it doesn't look like anything beyond professional friendship to me. At least not on his part."

"Is she pretty?"

"Not pretty like you. She's more the earth mother type."

Sunni wrinkled her nose. "Eww. Like she wears shapeless, unironed linen dresses and has her hair in Heidi braids?"

"No. Straight hair, blunt cut, to the middle of her back. Denim dresses and jumpers with little pictures stenciled along the hem."

"Which she probably sews and paints herself."

"That's Kristen." Jennifer looked up at the clock. "I have to finish up some paperwork so I can get out of here at a reasonable hour. Hot date tonight."

"Get going. And thanks for talking to me. I feel better."

I do feel better, Sunni thought after Jennifer was gone. It was nice to know the competition. Not that she was competing with Kristen for Teacher of the Year or for the heart of the principal. *No way.*

She just wanted to hang on to her job long enough to prove something to Mason. And no matter how good-looking Ethan was, Kristen was welcome to him, too. When Sunni settled down, it would be with a man who loved and appreciated her for who she was.

six

Seven o'clock sharp Monday morning, Sunni strode into Central Middle School a new woman. No longer satisfied merely to hang on to her job until the end of the year, she was determined to shine. She wasn't going to be the replacement for the Teacher of the Year. She was going to be the new Teacher of the Year.

And the man who caused her sudden change of heart was the same man who'd broken it.

Sunni had run into Mason at a party at her best friend Donna's house on Friday night. After Sunni had recovered from her initial shock of seeing Mason with his fiancée, she had walked over to greet the twosome, an extremely magnanimous gesture on her part. She had politely listened to them talk about things at their office; then she casually mentioned she had recently entered the workforce when her dream job of being a middle-school home ec teacher had finally opened up.

Mason had exploded into laughter. When he finally recovered his speech, several uncomfortable seconds later, he said he couldn't think of anything worse than Sunni teaching, and he wondered how long it would be before she burned down the school.

Sunni had blanched. How did he know?

As he continued to laugh at her, she realized he hadn't

discovered the humiliating facts about the fire alarm and was joking with her. She had laughed along with him to show him that, in addition to being a career woman with a fulfilling job, she had a terrific sense of humor.

She should have said her good-byes then and moved on to speak to someone else, but instead she lingered to tell Mason she'd found her purpose teaching young teens. When he stopped laughing, he told her he'd be surprised if her "purpose" lasted until the end of the semester.

That was when she decided she was going to be the best home ec teacher Central Middle School ever had.

To celebrate her decision, she swung by a craft store on the way home from the party and bought a glue gun.

Sunni'd had the whole weekend to plot her course. She'd stick with the curriculum she'd planned out, but she'd tweak it a bit. Even though the kids weren't prepared to cook, she would have to incorporate some other element into the classes besides lecturing. After her first week of school, Sunni's enthusiasm for lecturing on the four basic food groups had dimmed. According to Mr. Harris, if she wasn't excited, then she couldn't expect her students to be.

Beginning today, she'd add demonstrations or hands-on exercises to each class. She shifted the heavy grocery bag she carried. Today's demonstration involved hamburger meat.

Along with her work in the classroom, Sunni needed to do something for the faculty. Her predecessor, three-time Teacher of the Year Kristen Hobart, had regularly provided gourmet goodies for her fellow teachers to snack on.

No way was Sunni going to bring food. Even if she could prepare it, she doubted very much if the faculty would risk eating it. The unfortunate smoking-cookie incident hadn't instilled much confidence in her culinary expertise.

Sunni thought long and hard about what she could do for the others. What did they need that she could supply?

Money was her first thought. Teachers were notoriously underpaid, and she was rich. *No.* She couldn't very well tuck cash into their mailboxes. Her supply of money was not unlimited, and even if it was, she didn't want people to think she'd bought her way into Teacher of the Year.

Her second thought was that everyone needed affection. She could make it a point to hug each member of the staff everyday. She figured Coach Rawley would like it, but she wasn't too sure about the others. In the end, she decided distributing hugs wasn't practical.

A trip down the candy aisle of the drugstore Saturday morning gave Sunni the inspiration she sought. She'd bring everyone a foil-covered chocolate kiss every day. Not only would the staff know someone was thinking about them, she'd also be supplying everyone with chocolate—the unnamed yet most critical food group.

She decided to hot glue the chocolates to a file card with a short message written on it. After experimenting with "Have a nice day" and similar worn clichés, she took out a book of inspirational quotations someone had given her for graduation. She thumbed through the leather-bound book looking for a short and uplifting quote. Calvin Coolidge's "No man was ever honored for what he received. Honor has been the reward for what he gave" seemed to fit the bill.

She'd handwritten the cards Sunday night. It had taken her two hours, not counting the time it took to hot glue the candies onto the finished cards. She would have to streamline the process if she was going to do this on a regular basis.

Sunni's first stop Monday morning was the empty faculty lounge. She felt like Santa Claus as she tucked a candigram into each teacher's cubbyhole. She worked quickly. By the time the geography teacher walked in, Sunni was finished.

She hurried on to the home ec room with a light heart. It felt truly gratifying to do something unexpected for someone else. And if it bought brownie points for her, so much the better.

As soon as she arrived in her classroom and put the packages of meat in the front refrigerator, she called down to the office to request that the custodian deliver a table. A rather nicked linoleum-topped table arrived before her homeroom dismissed.

She greeted her first-period class with a smile. Their faces were becoming familiar to her. Occasionally she could connect a name to a face without checking the roster.

"It's good to see you all this morning." Sunni glanced toward the back of the room where the chair Mr. Harris had used last week now sat empty. "It's especially nice to be missing one all-too-familiar face."

The kids knew she referred to the principal who'd audited their class several times last week. They laughed.

"Today we're going to continue with our discussion of the four basic food groups. If you checked your syllabus, you'll see that we're going to concentrate on meats for a couple of days. Today we're talking about beef."

She lectured ten minutes about beef, starting with the nutritional value of red meat and ending with the USDA classifications.

She strode to the refrigerator in kitchen one and withdrew three of the butcher paper–wrapped packages. "One of the aims of home economics is to teach you how to plan and prepare nutritious meals on a budget. An economical way to incorporate beef into the menu is by using ground beef."

She carried the meat to the front table. "Federal regulations specify that ground beef be labeled according to how much fat is ground into the mix. I have here three different types."

She unwrapped the first package. "This is ground beef. The fat content is approximately thirty percent of the total volume."

She lifted the package to show the class. The smell of raw meat wafted under her nose. *Ugh.* It was all she could do not to gag. She studied the meat so she could describe it to the students who were sitting in the back. "It's very pink in color, and there appear to be bits of—oh, my, are those chopped-up blood vessels in there?"

She put the open package down quickly and moved on to number two. "This is ground chuck," she said as she unwrapped it. "It has a fat content of approximately twenty percent."

Instead of lifting it, she turned the package toward the class for them to see. She chanced a quick peek. "It's not as pink as the first package, and I can't see as many yucky bits of stuff chopped up in it."

Her stomach was roiling. Sunni was in such a hurry to finish with the nasty raw meat demonstration that she accidentally stuck her finger into the meat in package three. "This is low-fat beef, with the lowest fat content."

When she looked down and saw a hunk of raw meat wedged under her fingernail, her stomach did a slow twist.

Black dots appeared in front of her eyes. She blinked, but instead of disappearing, the dots multiplied.

"Hey," she heard someone say, "Miss Vanderclef is going to faint."

Yes, she thought in a weird, disembodied sort of way, *that is exactly what I'm going to do.* Vaguely grateful for having had the foresight to wear slacks, Sunni crumpled to the floor in a semiupright, cross-legged position.

"Make her put her head between her knees."

Sunni felt gentle pressure on the back of her neck, guiding her head down.

"Breathe deeply, Miss Vanderclef."

"Home ec is so great," someone said. "I mean, what other class offers fires and fainting?"

❧

Ethan Harris was determined to stay out of the home ec room. He was a busy man. He had a school to run. Another blue ribbon to earn. He had a thousand more pressing responsibilities than to babysit his newest teacher.

Actually he held out hope that after her rough start, Ms. Vanderclef might be getting the hang of the whole teacher thing. He hated to admit it, but her classroom style was pretty good. Despite her inexperience, she had a natural poise in front of her students. And if they lost interest in what she was saying, it was unlikely they'd get bored looking at her. Sunni was the prettiest teacher in the school. *In the district. Probably in the state.* That had to be the reason he'd showed up in her room three days in a row. He enjoyed looking at her.

At five past eight, he sat down at his computer and began

working on a report for the district that required him to input several pages of detailed data. He'd put off the report for a week, knowing it would take several hours of his full attention. The report was just the distraction he needed this morning to keep him from Sunni's classroom.

He emerged bleary-eyed from his office a little after eleven. "I finished the district report, Mrs. Leeper."

She smiled. "Good. I'm sure that's a load off your mind."

He was half afraid to ask. "What's been going on while I've been holed up?"

"Not much. Things always seem to settle down after the first week of school."

"You're right." Ethan was restless after sitting for so long. "I think I'll wander down to the cafeteria and see what the kids are doing. 'A' lunch should start any minute."

He felt a familiar sense of pride as he strolled down the main hall toward the cafeteria. Central Middle School was a model junior high. Though the building was thirty years old, it sparkled. The halls were clean and well lit; the floor tiles gleamed from a recent polishing. Colorful student artwork and inspirational posters lined the freshly painted walls.

Central hadn't always been a showplace. When he'd been assigned to the school three years ago, the youngest principal in the district, Central was in serious decline. The building was dirty, the students undisciplined, and teacher morale was at an all-time low.

Ethan remembered walking into the building for the very first time. It had felt as though he'd entered a war zone. He'd fought a very real temptation to turn and run. Others had told him the situation at Central was hopeless, and at that moment, looking at the grime and confusion, Ethan had believed it.

He might have quit that day if it hadn't been for the challenge his father had unwittingly issued.

"One man can't make a difference," his father had said. "The school system is tied up in red tape. Even someone as sharp as you can't cut through the bureaucracy. It'll smother you. One man can't make a difference."

But Ethan knew better.

A man called and equipped by God could accomplish great things regardless of the obstacles in his path.

His father's challenge, coupled with Ethan's faith, goaded Ethan into action. In the years since he joined Central Middle School, he had run up against some seemingly insurmountable bureaucratic walls. And each time, by the grace of God, he'd gone over the top of them.

Ethan had poured himself wholeheartedly into Central. It cost him everything—money, strength, a personal life—but as he looked around today, he had no regrets.

Through his sacrifice and that of his staff, they'd built a first-class institution of learning. Central students received an education second to none, in a clean, upbeat environment. He didn't know what the students would go on to make of their lives, but he knew he'd provided them with the best possible foundation to achieve future success.

His father had been wrong. One man could make a difference.

"Hi, Mr. Harris."

"Hi, Jarred. What's new?"

"Not much."

"How are classes going?"

"Great. We had a really cool home ec class today. Miss Vanderclef fainted."

Ethan felt a bit light-headed himself. "She what?"

"Fainted," Jarred confirmed with a delighted smile. "Fell down in a heap. One minute, she's talking about hamburger, and the next minute, she's out. It was so great."

One woman could also make a difference. She could single-handedly undo all the good he'd given his life to accomplish.

Neither Mrs. Leeper nor Ms. Vanderclef seemed surprised by the summons to his office immediately after school.

"Hi, Mrs. Leeper," Sunni said on her way in. "Any idea what I'm in trouble for today?"

Mrs. Leeper frowned and shook her head. "None." Her face brightened. "Maybe he just wants to tell you what a great job you're doing. The halls are buzzing with the word that your class is the most interesting one at Central."

"Uh-oh."

Ethan heard Sunni's voice outside his office and went to the door to invite her in. "Come in, Ms. Vanderclef. Tell me about your day."

The urge to strangle her wasn't so strong today, but he positioned himself on the other side of his desk, just in case. She looked lovely, as always. Her color looked good, but of course she'd had several hours to recover from her faint.

"I suppose you heard about my little fainting episode."

Ethan nodded. "It was mentioned once or twice." *A minute.* Sunni's collapse had been the talk of the school. The football team's first win of the season was nothing compared to a teacher keeling over.

She frowned. "I hope you're not mad. It's not like I intended to faint."

She must really think he was an ogre. "No, I'm not mad. I'm concerned."

Her lips turned up at the corners. "Oh. That's nice. You don't need to worry. It was a freak thing. I didn't eat breakfast this morning because I had to run to the grocery store and pick up meat for my class. I was showing the kids the different classifications of ground beef, and I accidentally got some stuck under my fingernail. The combination of an empty stomach, the raw meat smell, and the sight of a cold, bloody glob of it under my nail—and I hit the floor."

"You've never seen raw hamburger before?"

She shook her head. "Not up close. And I don't recommend it. You can't imagine the disgusting stuff I saw mixed in with the meat. Just thinking about it makes me woozy."

Ethan was on his feet. "Sit down," he commanded.

Sunni laughed as she took a seat. "You really are concerned."

"Yeah. I'm not up-to-date on my first aid if you decide to faint again."

"The kids were great. They knew exactly what to do. They said Coach Rawley teaches a unit on basic first aid. He stopped by at lunch to say he'd be happy to give me a private course."

"I'll bet. Complete with a lesson in mouth-to-mouth resuscitation."

Sunni laughed and nodded. "Does that mean I'm not the first person he's tried that on?"

Ethan shook his head. "Nope. Jerry's pretty consistent. He offers his services to all new attractive females."

"I'll take that as a compliment."

"Take it as a warning. He's a nice guy, but he considers himself a real ladies' man."

"Did he hit on Kristen?"

The question took Ethan by surprise. "Ms. Hobart? I don't know? Why do you ask?"

She shrugged. "Just curious."

"While we're talking about other teachers," Ethan said, "let me say I thought the card with the candy was a nice idea."

"You did? How'd you know about it?"

"You mean, how did I know about it since I didn't get one in my box?"

Sunni looked guilty.

"You forget, Ms. Vanderclef—I know everything."

"That's right. You did mention principals are omniscient."

"Exactly. I thought it was kind of you to distribute the candy. Several of the faculty mentioned it to me. Seems you made their day."

She looked pleased. "I'm glad."

It was a nice change to be making her glad instead of sad. The smile she leveled on him almost knocked the air out of his lungs.

She was watching him expectantly. He knew he didn't have a good reason to detain her further, other than he liked to look at her.

"Okay," he said at last, "that's all I needed to talk about with you."

"I can go?"

"Absolutely."

"You're not going to lecture me?"

"Nope."

"Wow. I guess I'll get out of here before you change your mind."

As she reached for the door, he said, "Wait. Haven't we forgotten something?"

"What's that?"

"My professional advice for the day."

"Okay. What is it?"

"Keep up the good work."

seven

Keep up the good work.

Mr. Harris had actually told her to keep up the good work. He approved of what she was doing.

Sunni was ecstatic. Part of the reason was that she couldn't win Teacher of the Year without the principal's backing, but beyond that, it was nice to know he was beginning to see her as something other than a menace.

He'd smiled at her when she left his office yesterday afternoon. Not the usual baring of teeth he thought passed for pleasant, but a full-blown smile that lit up his face. *His very handsome face.* She hadn't appreciated his heart-stopping good looks before now, probably because he'd usually spoiled them with a sneer.

Suddenly she could see why the single teachers fell all over him. She wondered if he smiled at Kristen in the same way he'd smiled at her yesterday. The full smile that did funny things to her insides. She didn't know why, but she hoped he didn't. She hoped he saved his special melting smile all for her.

As Sunni set up her classroom the following day before school, she wondered if Ethan Harris would ever smile at her again. She had an inkling he might not be thrilled with the special program she'd planned for her students.

To be Teacher of the Year, she had to be out of the ordinary. Since her talents didn't lean toward milk-carton sculpting or beaded cats, she had to content herself with excelling in the classroom. She'd committed to offering her students more than a boring lecture. She was going to give them live demonstrations to help make the material she was teaching come to life.

It seemed like the perfect plan until she fainted over the hamburger. How would she ever survive the chicken and pork lessons?

She needed backup. Somebody to touch the slimy yellow chickens waiting in the refrigerator. She needed Ramon.

Ramon Ducre had worked for her family for years. A Paris-trained chef, the man was a genius in the kitchen. More important to Sunni, he didn't flinch at the sight of a little raw meat.

She personally thought her plan to bring in Ramon was a brilliant one. She'd introduce him as a guest speaker and let him hack up the chickens into economical cuts. The kids would get an interesting demonstration, and she wouldn't disgrace herself by fainting. If only she could be sure Mr. Harris would see her plan in the same positive light.

She knew it was too much to hope Mr. Harris wouldn't find out, so instead she hoped he wouldn't find out until the end of the day. He might fuss a bit, but she was used to that. There was always the off chance he'd like her plan. He might even flash her one of those smiles and tell her to keep up the good work.

When the buzzer rang, signaling the end of homeroom, Sunni slipped down the hall to the back door that led to the outside. As arranged, Ramon waited there for her.

Smiling, she pushed open the door. "Right on time. Follow me."

She led him down the short stretch of hall, and after

pausing to check for signs of Mr. Harris, she led him around the corner to her classroom.

"Go ahead and arrange everything on the front table," she told him. "It'll take me a few minutes to set the stage, and then I'll turn the program over to you."

Ramon laid out his knives and cutting boards while Sunni took care of the roll and daily announcements.

"As you can see, I've invited a special guest today. Chef Ramon is here to help us learn about incorporating chicken in our diets."

"Will he faint?" some unidentified smart aleck called from the back.

"Ha-ha," Sunni said with a repressive glare. "Ramon, would you like to tell us a little bit about yourself?"

His intriguing accent and crisp white uniform complete with tall hat captured the class's attention. Sunni positioned herself on the stool in front of the class several feet to the right of the table where Ramon worked. She'd chosen the spot so she and Ramon could share center stage as the program would shift between the two of them, but also so she was enough removed from the raw meat that she wouldn't be sick.

The class went off without a hitch, even better than she had hoped. Ramon was not only talented, but he was entertaining. The kids loved his sense of humor, and at the end of class, they gave him a warm round of applause.

As they gathered up their books and backpacks in anticipation of the dismissal buzzer, Sunni said, "I don't want you to mention Ramon to anyone outside this class. That way he'll be a nice surprise for all the other home ec students."

Second period began like the first. The kids took to Ramon immediately. Sunni lectured. Ramon chopped. At one point, when Ramon picked up his meat cleaver to chop the poor chicken in two, Sunni turned her face toward the door. That's when she saw Mr. Harris standing in the hall, just out of sight of the class.

Uh-oh. She would have ignored him if he hadn't been flailing his arms, signaling her to join him in the hall.

"Please continue, Ramon. I'm going to step out into the hall for a second."

Sunni noted that Mr. Harris wasn't wearing his "good work" smile. True to form, he didn't waste time with pleasantries. "Who is that man?" he hissed.

"What man?"

He actually growled. "The man in the white coat. The one waving a meat cleaver like a scimitar."

Sunni tried for cheery casual. "Oh, *that* man. That's Ramon."

"What is Ramon doing in your classroom?"

"He's helping me teach about chicken."

The veins were bulging in Mr. Harris's nicely tanned neck. "You can't bring a strange man in here. A strange, armed man."

"Ramon's not strange. He's a chef. He works for my family. I've known him all my life."

"Did you clear him through the front office?"

"Was I supposed to?" She knew that sounded lame, but truly the security issue had never occurred to her.

Applause spilled out from the home ec room. "They like him," Sunni said.

Mr. Harris had that scary homicidal-maniac smile on again. "How nice. Will Ramon and his knives be with us all day?"

"That was the plan."

"Fine. After you pack him off at the end of the day, I want to see you in my office. Do you understand?"

She understood she'd been demoted back to "menace."

"Yes, sir."

"Then get back in there. And keep those knives away from the kids."

ِ❧

"Mr. Harris, you have a call on line three. Kristen Hobart."

"Thank you, Mrs. Leeper. I'll take it in my office. I need to sit down."

He pushed the door closed and slumped back against it. He'd almost fainted. When he saw a stranger waving a twelve-inch knife, his joints had turned to jelly. The only thing that kept him from flopping onto the floor was anger.

And he was plenty angry. How could she do it? Deep down, he knew she wouldn't endanger her class, but she should have known to clear something like this through him.

The light on his phone flickered. *Kristen!*

He scooped up the receiver. "Hi, Kristen. Sorry to keep you waiting."

"No problem. You're a busy man. I hope I'm not bothering you."

"Not at all. It's nice to speak to a rational human being."

"That sounds ominous. Trouble?"

"Ha! That's an understatement. I've got Sunni Vanderclef. She's worse than trouble."

"What has she done now?"

"What hasn't she done? She takes personal calls in class and invites family friends to help her teach. She's a menace."

"She doesn't sound particularly menacing," Kristen soothed. "Of course, she doesn't sound much like a teacher either."

"You're full of understatements today. I don't think she has a clue about what it means to be a teacher. I thought she was catching on. At one point, I believed she could pull it off, but I was wrong." Ethan was surprised to feel sorrow at the discovery. "Enough about me. How are you feeling?"

"Better. Everything's still broken, but I'm not in pain."

"I'm glad to hear it. I hate to rush you, but you've got to heal fast. I need you back at Central."

Kristen laughed. "Sure, boss. I'll get right on it."

≈

A vague sense of sadness hovered over Ethan all day. He'd thought he'd glimpsed something in Sunni, that spark of wonder he looked for in all his teachers. The indefinable passion common to the best of teachers.

After observing her in class, he had begun to believe he'd been hasty in his initial judgment of her. That there was more to Sunni than a spoiled rich girl looking for a way to pass the time. That she, like him, wanted to make a difference.

Then, just when she'd changed his mind, she pulled a stunt like this. Completely disregarding school policies to hire someone to teach her class. It made him angry to think he'd been fooled. She wasn't a teacher—she was playing school.

"Why, Lord?" he prayed. "Why did You send Sunni to Central Middle? Have I done something wrong, failed You in some way that You're punishing me?" He sighed. "You know I want to be faithful to You. I want to follow Your direction and act as Your hands and feet here. I told You I'm willing to learn whatever it is You want to teach me. But I can't let her destroy the school. I have to believe I missed Your will that day I hired her. So unless I get a direct sign from You, I'm going to fire her today."

Ethan scrubbed his hands over his face. The facts were clear; Sunni had to go.

The more he thought about this morning's stunt with the chef, the angrier he got. By the time Sunni showed up in front of his desk, looking every inch the country club girl with her expensive suit and high-heeled shoes, he'd worked up a good head of mad.

"Close the door, Ms. Vanderclef," he said. "Sit down. We need to talk."

Something in his tone or perhaps the fact he'd invited her to sit alerted Sunni to his feelings. Her sorority girl smile faded to a worried shadow as she took a seat across from him.

"If this is about Ramon," she said, "I'm sorry. I didn't think about the security issue."

"I'm sure you didn't," Ethan said. "Because that would mean you had to think about something besides yourself and what pleases you. But since district policies on security are so disinteresting to you, let's talk about something I know you'll be interested in. Let's talk about you. What were you thinking when you brought in a professional chef to your classroom? Do you plan to invite him back every day until the end of the semester? Does your family keep a seamstress on retainer that you can bring in for the second half of the year when you're supposed to teach sewing?"

"You don't understand."

Ethan sat forward, propping his forearms on the desk. "I understand plenty. I understand that a woman in your position is accustomed to buying her way through life. Why exert yourself when you can pay someone else to do it for you?"

Sunni stiffened. "That is completely unfair. This is not about money. This is about expertise. I'm teaching a unit about meats, a subject I know very little about. Ramon, on the other hand, makes his living by preparing food. Why shouldn't my students get the benefit of his experience?"

Ethan arched his brow. "So you did this solely for the benefit of your students."

She backed down. "Not completely. . ."

"Why didn't you just read the material and gain a level of competency so you could teach the class?"

"You know as well as I do that this is not about reading the textbook. This is about disgusting raw meat and fainting."

"So leave the actual meat out of it. Get a poster. Point to the pictures while you lecture." Ethan sighed. He'd gotten off track. He wasn't supposed to be giving her teaching tips. He was supposed to be firing her. "Tell me something, Ms. Vanderclef. Why did you go into teaching? And don't tell me it was because you thought it would be an easy major and a good way to pass the time while you waited to find Mr. Right and get married."

The expression on her face told him that was exactly why she was an education major. "Okay," he said, "forget I asked. Let me ask you something else. Regardless of your reason for studying education in college, why did you walk into Central and apply for a job? What did you expect to accomplish?"

She shrugged. "I wanted a job."

"Then you came to the wrong place. Teaching isn't a job. Teaching is a profession, probably the most demanding, draining profession in the world. It isn't about punching a clock or collecting a paycheck. It's about challenging a mind, changing a life. As a teacher, you have the means to influence these kids for good. But in order to influence them, you must invest yourself. And I don't mean financially. I mean investing what's inside you."

Sunni spent a long moment studying her hands. Finally

she lifted her gaze to his. "I want to teach," she said, then gave a self-deprecating chuckle. "I actually told myself I was going to be the very best teacher at Central Middle School. Teacher of the Year. I must have been delusional. I'm willing to invest in the kids, but I don't think I have what it takes inside."

This was his chance. She'd handed him a perfect excuse to fire her. Not that he needed one. Nobody in the world would blame him for booting her out.

He pushed back in his chair. He was formulating the words in his mind when suddenly, clearly, he could see Sunni for who she was. It was as if blinders had been removed from his eyes. Beyond the perfect hair and expensive clothes, beyond the family name and mountains of money, here was a woman of enormous worth. Properly channeled, her energy and enthusiasm could make a difference in the life of a child. In the clarity of the inspired moment, he knew he couldn't rob her of her chance to try.

"I disagree. I think you have a unique God-given gift, something beyond being rich. I believe you have something to contribute to this school, something you do better than anyone else. Your job is to find it." He paused to give her a hard, searching look. "I'm serious, Sunni. If you want to keep your position at Central, you must find your talent and use it. Find a need and fill it."

❧

Sunni picked up the phone on the fourth ring.

"Sunni? What are you doing? I thought I'd see you at the Douglasses' this evening."

Sunni looked around her now-dark living room in confusion. "Oh, hi, Mom, did I miss it? What time is it?"

"It's after ten. What's the matter? Did I wake you? Are you sick?"

"No. I've just been sitting here. I must have lost track of the time."

"You're working too hard, Sunni. Your father and I both think it's so cute that you have a job, but I don't think it's worth keeping if it's going to be demanding."

"Teaching isn't just a job. It's a profession."

"I'm sure you're right, dear."

"Mom, do you think I have a God-given gift? You know, something I do better than anyone else?"

Her mother chuckled. "Of course you do. You're one of the most gifted people I know. Who else has your knack for fashion? I've lost count of the number of times you've been on the best-dressed list on the society page. And think about how well you decorate. People are forever asking your advice on wallpaper and upholstery fabric."

"Those aren't exactly the kinds of gifts I'm talking about. I'm thinking of a gift I could share with others. Like being a gourmet cook or a wonderful singer."

"You're certainly not a gifted cook, no offense, dear. Your voice is nice. . . ." Her mother's voice trailed off.

Sunni's heart sank. "So what you're saying is that I don't have any gifts at all."

"I didn't say that. Besides, cooking and singing aren't gifts; they're accomplishments. You have many accomplishments; those just don't happen to be two of them. You're an accomplished hostess—"

Sunni began to feel desperate. "But what about gifts? Do I have a unique talent? Do I do *anything* better than anyone else?"

"You have a real talent for making people feel at ease. You make friends very easily."

"I don't think that's a talent."

"Of course it is. Being cheerful and personable, making the other person comfortable, is a wonderful talent and as natural to you as breathing. Everybody likes you."

"I should introduce you to my boss," Sunni muttered.

"What?"

"Never mind. Thanks, Mom. I appreciate your help. I need to hang up now so I can look over my lesson plans before I go to bed."

"Don't overdo, honey. No job is worth wearing yourself out."

Sunni switched off the phone and sighed. She'd been pondering Mr. Harris's ultimatum all afternoon. "If you want to keep your job, you must find your God-given talent and use it." So far, she'd come up blank. *Zilch. Nothing. Nada.* She could not identify one single talent. And if that wasn't depressing enough, her mother, the person who knew her best and loved her most, couldn't name one either.

Sunni scooted from her chair to her knees, turning so she could rest her elbows on the seat cushion. A tear trailed down her cheek as she bowed her head and prayed. "Oh, Lord, help me. I want to keep my job. I really do want to make a difference in children's lives. I want my life to count for something, but I don't know how."

She sighed. "This is getting to be a habit, isn't it? I wait until I've made a mess, and then I ask You to bail me out." Sunni's voice broke. "I want my walk with You to be more than a series of 9-1-1 calls, but I can't seem to change. Please help me. Change me."

She brushed away the tears that were falling freely now. "Mr. Harris says You gave me a talent, but I don't know what it is. And I'm half afraid he's wrong, that I'm not good at anything that matters. So if You don't mind, could You show me what it is You've gifted me to do? I promise that if You show me, then whatever it is, I'll use it to Your glory. Amen."

eight

Sunni continued to replay her meeting with Mr. Harris in her mind. She'd known the second he opened his mouth that he was going to fire her. He hadn't been just mad; he had been homicidal. In fact, if there was a step beyond homicidal, he was at it.

She'd expected the angry lecture; she'd deserved the biting remarks, but she'd been floored by the resolution. Instead of marching her out the double front doors of Central Middle School with a police escort, he'd told her, almost tenderly, that she had a unique gift to share with her students.

When he told her to identify her gift and use it, the strangest sensation came over her. She'd felt as if the heavens had opened and she'd received some sort of holy commission. At the time, his words had sent a jolt of energy shooting straight through her. Now, a day later, the memory gave her goose bumps.

The challenge he'd issued consumed her. He thought she had something valuable to contribute, and he wasn't talking about money. This went beyond being Teacher of the Year. He wanted her to be the best teacher she could be. To find a need and fill it.

She was willing to invest herself, to pour out her gift on her students. If only she knew what it was. She'd asked God to show her. Now all she had to do was watch and wait for His answer.

As she sat in the cafeteria, pondering the question, Jennifer walked over to her table. "Hi. Mind if I join you?"

Sunni smiled. "Be my guest."

"Where's your lunch?" Jennifer asked as she plopped her tray onto the table.

"I don't eat on the days when I have cafeteria duty." She wrinkled her nose. "It's the smell. The combination of the grease and entrée du jour kinda makes me sick. I don't know how the kids do it."

Jennifer laughed as she shoveled a forkful of mysterious casserole into her mouth. "I used to be like that. It took me a couple of years before I could stomach the smell enough to eat the lunch I brought from home. And another year before I worked up the courage to eat something they served here. Just wait—one day you'll find yourself craving whatever this is I'm eating."

Sunni eyed the plate skeptically. "If I last that long."

Jennifer looked at her. "What's the matter? Trouble with Ethan again?"

"Not yet, but there will be if I don't come up with a gift."

"A gift? Excellent strategy, girlfriend. You're going to bribe him."

Sunni laughed. "Not that kind of gift. I mean, gift like talent. Mr. Harris says everybody has a unique talent and that I need to find mine and use it. Or else."

"That's easy. You're an encourager. And friendly. Everybody says so."

Friendship again. Was this some kind of confirmation from God? "Thank you, but do you honestly believe that's a talent?"

"Absolutely."

"Okay. So how do I use it?"

Jennifer hesitated. "Hmm. Good question. I guess you go around saying nice, friendly things to people."

All afternoon, Sunni concentrated on saying nice, friendly things to people. She was nice to the giggly seventh-grade boys who wrote their names on the cafeteria wall with squeeze packets of catsup. Instead of sending the herd of them down to Mr. Harris, she smiled her widest, friendliest smile while handing out paper towels and spray cleaner. She continued to smile while explaining in her friendliest tones that the next time they made a mess like that they would be cleaning it up with their tongues.

She stood in the doorway after her fourth-period class and sent each student out with a compliment or an encouraging word. Because she knew it was important to their self-esteem, she was careful to call each child by name, even getting a few of them right.

She was nice to Coach Rawley when he showed up in her classroom during her free period. Sunni frowned. The lecherous coach really stretched her ability to be nice.

When the first bell for sixth period rang, Sunni stood in the doorway to await her last class. As she had all day, she watched the milling students, looking for the need God wanted her to fill.

Things in the hall looked much the same as they did every day. Noise swelled as the students hurried toward their next classes. Junior high kids tended to travel in packs. Groups of three or four would walk together, laughing and talking, or calling out greetings to other packs.

Each pack appeared to be composed of similar students. Jocks stuck together; cheerleaders moved as one unit joined at the hip; the more studious kids found their own cliques. Sunni supposed there was some sociological reason for the group compositions—"like attracting like" or something.

The students not traveling in packs tended to travel in pairs, boys with boys, girls with girls. Sunni figured these were best friends who didn't want to join the larger groups.

Occasionally Sunni saw a single student navigating the crowded halls alone. These kids didn't laugh and call out to the others. Instead, they kept their heads bowed and their books clutched protectively to their chests as they scurried along the fringes.

It was to these people, the loners, that her attention was drawn that afternoon. She wondered if they were alone because they chose to be or because nobody wanted to be with them. Why were these kids excluded?

A boy brushed past her, alone. She followed his progress down the hall, trying to see what, if anything, was different about the young man. He was small for a junior high student. His complexion was bad, and his haircut was awful. His clothing, jeans and a T-shirt like everyone else's, didn't look trendy, just sloppy. He kept his gaze trained on the floor as he hurried along.

As she lost sight of him, another boy passed. He, too, was alone, but he didn't rush along. He moseyed down the hall as though he had all the time in the world. Instead of concentrating on his feet, he kept his eyes up. The expression on his face looked pleasant, almost expectant, as if he were waiting for someone to notice him. No one did.

"Hi, Miss Vanderclef."

"Hello, Amanda." Sunni stepped aside to allow the eighth grader to enter the classroom.

Amanda was a loner. Sunni noticed from the very first class that Amanda didn't have anyone to talk to. While the others chatted among themselves as they waited for the buzzer to ring, Amanda sat quietly at her desk. Sunni had assumed Amanda was a neat freak the way she arranged her notebook and pens just so, but today it occurred to her that perhaps Amanda fussed with her supplies to cover the fact that no one spoke to her. To make it look as if she were too busy to talk.

Sunni wondered why Amanda didn't have any friends. She seemed like a nice girl. She was quiet, maybe shy, but she had a nice smile. She did wear an enormous amount of makeup, enough for a circus performer, but that was no reason to shun her.

The buzzer rang, calling the class to order. Sunni continued her lecture on meats with the help of some large posters she found in the home ec closet, but her mind was miles away from pork chops and ham.

A light seemed to have gone off in her head. If she heard God right, then her dubious talent was friendliness. Could she use her gift in some way to help these kids who had no friends? Was this a need she could fill?

Time seemed to drag. Sunni caught herself watching the clock during the last fifteen minutes of class, wishing the buzzer would sound so she could stop talking about cold cuts and begin planning and praying about how she could work in the lives of these kids.

The students must have noticed her preoccupation with the clock. They, too, seemed to spend an inordinate amount of time watching it.

"What's the matter?" Sunni asked when it became obvious

she no longer had the attention of the class. "Am I boring you?"

A boy in the front row acted as spokesman. "It's ten minutes till three."

Sunni was puzzled. "So?"

"So how come nobody's called down from the office to tell you to report to Mr. Harris after school?"

The class laughed.

Sunni felt her face heat. They hadn't been watching the clock because they were anxious to get out of class. They were waiting for her customary summons. She'd been in trouble every single day since she'd begun teaching, but she hadn't realized her students knew it.

She shrugged and tried to laugh it off. "I guess I'm just lucky."

"Aw, Miss Vanderclef, we thought you were going to break the record for most consecutive trips to the principal's office. Tony Barto held the record up till now. He went six days in a row. If you got called in today, it'd be seven."

No point in being embarrassed. Her kids thought the reprimands made her a celebrity. It occurred to Sunni that it might be nice to talk over her newly formed friendship plan with Mr. Harris.

"Does it count if I call down there and ask to see Mr. Harris?" she asked.

After some debate, the class decided that a trip to the principal's office was a trip to the principal's office, regardless of who initiated it.

She pressed the intercom button and waited for Mrs. Leeper to answer. "Hi, Mrs. Leeper. Does Mr. Harris have any free time to see me in his office this afternoon?"

The long pause on the other end indicated Mrs. Leeper

was surprised by Sunni's request. "Let me check, dear."

Seconds later, Mrs. Leeper called back. "That's fine. Mr. Harris will see you in his office after class."

"Thanks, Mrs. Leeper."

The class cheered after she disconnected.

❧

Mr. Harris was waiting for her. He sat behind his desk, his hands folded on top.

He didn't look like wrathful Jehovah. His dark eyes sparkled, but not with the unnatural glow of banked anger. Today they looked lively and intelligent. And curious.

His posture was relaxed. He'd loosened his tie, resulting in a warm disheveled sort of look. He looked friendly and approachable.

"This is a surprise," he said.

"I don't know why. I've been in here every day."

"Yes, but not by choice."

Sunni frowned. "Didn't your mother teach you that it's in poor taste to bring up the past sins of others?"

"Probably." He raised his hands in a conciliating gesture. "Okay, forget I said that. So what brings you here today? Some new crisis I didn't hear about? A plague that has yet to reach my ears?"

"Very funny. I thought you were going to forget."

"Can I help it if I have a memory like an elephant?"

"Evidently not." She took the seat across from him. "Isn't it possible I just wanted to talk?"

He seemed to consider. "Possible, yes. Likely, no."

"It's true. I had an idea about what we talked about yesterday, and I wanted to run it by you."

"Okay, shoot."

"Remember when you told me to find my unique gift?"

"Yes. I confess I'm surprised you remember. I didn't think you were listening."

She frowned at him. "Are you trying to be tacky?"

"No," he said with a grin. "It comes naturally."

"I don't think tackiness is a good quality in a principal. You're supposed to set an example for the rest of us. Anyway, for your information, I was listening. I've been giving it a lot of thought. I've prayed about it, and I've talked with several unbiased third parties to get their opinions. The consensus is that my talent is friendliness."

He just looked at her.

"I can see you're underwhelmed. I'm not offended because frankly I was, too. Friendly doesn't seem like much of a gift. But, such as it is, it's all I've got. And I promised God I'd do something with it. You told me to find a need and fill it. There are kids in this school without friends, and I'm going to do something about it."

"*You're* going to be their friend?"

"No. I'm going to start a club so they can make their own friends."

He didn't seem to recognize the genius in her plan. "They're a bit young for sororities, don't you think?"

"I wasn't talking about starting a sorority. I'm talking about a club. For boys and girls. The Club."

He appeared to warm slightly to the idea. "It's true some kids here don't seem to have a place to belong. It's a problem with schools everywhere. But I don't see what good it will do to have a club. The kinds of kids we're talking about—disenfranchised kids—don't join clubs."

"They'll join this one."

He cocked a brow. "How do you figure that?"

"I'll invite them personally. I'm not naive enough to think it will work for everyone, but I'm counting on the fact that some of them would join if somebody went to the trouble to ask them."

"I suppose it's worth a try."

"Of course it is. Once the popular kids get to know these loners in a social setting, they'll start to include them in the popular activities. My guess is that the popular kids aren't deliberately leaving them out. It's more that they are so wrapped up in their own circles that they don't notice the loners."

"I bet you were always part of the popular crowd."

Sunni nodded. "I was. Cheerleader, homecoming queen, sorority officer—I did it all. And you may as well wipe that disapproving look off your face because I can't believe you were ever disenfranchised."

"Why not?"

"Look at you. Attractive men do not end up disenfranchised. They are worshipped." She could see him puff up with the compliment and decided to bring him down a peg for all the harassment he'd given her. "And barring an anger-management problem, you seem to have an okay personality."

"I do not have an anger-management problem."

"Is that what your therapist tells you?" she asked with an almost-straight face. "It's probably a good idea for you to keep repeating it. Positive reinforcement can be a powerful thing."

His voice rose an octave. "I don't have a therapist—"

Sunni wagged a finger at him. "Uh-oh. I'm detecting a little anger surfacing."

He caught himself. In a second, he was laughing and shaking his head. "What did I ever do to deserve you, Ms. Vanderclef?"

She smiled. "I guess you must've been very good."

nine

When Sunni heard the classroom door creak open, she ducked behind the refrigerator in kitchen six.

"Ms. Vanderclef? Are you in here?"

Whew. It was only Mr. Harris. She popped her head out. "I'm back here," she called in a loud whisper. "Come on in. And close the door behind you."

She waited until the door closed before stepping out from her hiding place. "Hi."

"Hi, yourself. It's so dark in here I almost didn't stop. I figured you'd gone home." He reached out to flick on the overhead lights in the front of the classroom.

"No! Don't turn them on." Sunni waved him toward the back. "It's light back here."

He laughed at her odd behavior. "What are you doing? Hiding?"

She nodded. "I didn't want Coach Jerry to know I was in here, so I cut off the front lights and am working in the back of the room."

"Has he been bothering you?"

"Yes, he's been bothering me. He won't leave me alone."

"You want me to talk to him?"

"I wish I thought it would help. It'd be like asking him not to breathe."

"He won't be breathing if I find out he's been harassing you."

The unexpected protectiveness was nice. "Thanks. I think

96

he's harmless. Actually I'm not sure I didn't start the trouble when I sent him my little candigram."

"Speaking of which, I got mine. Thanks."

She'd included Mr. Harris in the second round of inspirational notes stuck in faculty mailboxes after he'd sounded so disappointed about being left out of the first "mailing." "You're welcome."

"If it's okay with you, I thought I'd use the quotation in the morning announcements. Like a thought for the day. Since the staff is all talking about how motivational the quotes are, I thought the kids might enjoy them, too."

"That's nice. I'd be glad for you to use them."

In the unusual moment of harmony, their gazes met and held. Sunni's smile faltered as the intensity built between them. For one breathless second as his gaze shifted to her mouth, she thought he would kiss her. Her body swayed toward his.

His head lowered. Sunni waited, her heart hammering against her ribs.

Suddenly he seemed to come to his senses. He took a step back and shoved his hands in his pockets. His voice was shaky. "So what are you working on back here?"

It took Sunni longer to recover. Her gaze stayed focused on his mouth. She wondered what it would have been like to kiss him. She sighed. "What?"

The corners of his mouth turned up in a grin. "I asked what you are doing."

Besides making a fool of myself with my boss? Other than fantasizing about kissing the principal? She gave herself a good mental shake. "I'm making posters for the first meeting of the Club."

She walked to the counter and picked up the top poster and held it out for his inspection. "What do you think?"

"Be a charter member of the Club," he read aloud. "Everyone welcome. Join us for our first meeting, Friday at 3:00, in the home ec room. Refreshments will be served—" He broke off, lifting alarmed eyes to hers. "You're not cooking, are you?"

She dropped the poster back on the stack. "Very funny."

"Do you hear me laughing? I need to know if I should put the fire department on alert."

"No, you should not," she snapped, "although I'm tempted to cook just to prove to you I'm capable. Unfortunately I don't have time to get everything done and bake snacks before the meeting on Friday. Ramon is doing the cooking for me."

He let out a noisy breath. "What a relief to have Ramon!"

"There you go being tacky again."

"I told you—it comes naturally."

"Did you seek me out this afternoon for the express purpose of insulting me?" Sunni asked.

"Actually I came by to bring you the bylaws you dropped off for me to look at. I thought they looked great."

"Really?"

"Yeah. It looks like you've covered just about everything."

"Just about everything?" She frowned. "What did I miss?"

"I didn't see anything about collecting dues."

Sunni shrugged. "That's because I'm not."

"What are you going to use to cover expenses?"

"My own money."

Mr. Harris shook his head. "Clubs don't work that way."

"Mine does. And before you start lecturing me about trying to buy my way through life, let me explain. I listen to the announcements every day. Nearly every activity at this school costs money. Two dollars here. Five dollars there. It all adds up. Suppose somebody wanted to join the Club but couldn't afford to pay dues. It would break my heart if money stood in the way of someone making a friend."

"Have scholarships available for kids who don't have the money," he suggested.

"What is the likelihood that anyone would come forward to collect a scholarship? Since these disenfranchised kids seem to hang back, why provide them with another obstacle to overcome?"

"I don't like it."

She took a step forward, putting herself right in his face. "I'm rich, Mr. Harris. Like it or not, I have more money than I could ever spend in ten lifetimes. I know you think money is a liability, but I think it's a gift. It frees me to do things for other people."

"I never said money was a liability."

"Maybe not, but on several occasions, you have implied that being rich is worse than having leprosy."

"I don't have anything against being rich."

Her brows shot up. "You could have fooled me."

"If I seem a bit prejudiced against wealthy people, it's because my experience with them has been very bad."

"Okay, tell me about these terrible rich people."

"Don't put words in my mouth. They're not terrible. They are selfish. They're so wrapped up in their gilded, privileged world that they refuse to see there's a world outside that needs their help."

Even though she disagreed with him, she could see he was serious. She looked into his eyes. "Maybe I'm different."

He considered her for a long moment, then smiled. "Maybe you are."

❧

Sunni Vanderclef was different all right. Just about the time Ethan thought he had her figured out, she'd do something to change his mind.

He'd originally pegged her as a spoiled socialite playing school. That perception held until he'd witnessed her in the classroom. When he saw that touch of wonder in her as she worked with her students, he'd been ready to admit he'd been wrong about her and that she had all the makings of a fine teacher.

No sooner than he'd decided she wasn't half bad, she went and hired a chef to take over her classes. That incident confirmed his original assessment—Sunni Vanderclef was a little rich girl playing school.

He didn't know why he'd bothered to give her the lecture about finding her gift and using it. He'd been pretty sure she tuned the whole thing out as just another one of his displays of bad temper.

But she'd been listening. And soul-searching. It was too early to tell if she had what it took to follow through on her good intentions, but he believed she honestly wanted to serve the kids.

Without conscious planning, he found himself at the door of the semidarkened home ec room the next day after school. He looked both ways down the hall before slipping through the door and closing it tightly behind him.

"Ms. Vanderclef?"

"Oh! Hi, Mr. Harris," Sunni called from the back. "I'm hiding out in kitchen six again. Come on back."

He found her putting the finishing touches on yet another poster. "Are you making more?"

"Uh-huh. After I hung the others yesterday, I realized I didn't have great coverage in A Hall. I thought I'd make a couple more to hang by the entrances." She lifted a poster to him. "What do you think? Catchy enough?"

Like all the posters she'd created, this was a work of art. She'd obviously spent hours on the fancy lettering and more hours gluing sparkly glitter in strategic places. "It looks like an attention-grabber to me."

She looked from the poster to him and smiled. "I hope so."

"You've done a good job getting the word out. Between posters and commercials during the morning announcements, there can't be a student at Central who doesn't know about the Club."

She caught her lip between her teeth. "But will they come?"

The flash of insecurity touched him. He wanted to place a comforting hand on her shoulder or, better yet, pull her into his arms but decided to bury his hands in his pockets instead.

He knew the drill. Principals needed to maintain a professional distance between themselves and their staff. The fact that he was attracted to Sunni made it all the more imperative he keep his hands to himself.

This was a new problem for him. He'd grown accustomed to female teachers hitting on him when he was in the classroom, and even now as a principal, but he'd never been interested. Beyond the fact that workplace relationships were dangerous at best, none of the women appealed to him. *Until Sunni.*

Why he should be attracted to a woman who had tried to

burn down his school remained a mystery. Unlike most single female teachers who went out of their way to be accommodating and pleasant to him, Sunni appeared to be determined to drive him nuts.

She wasn't awed by his authority. She challenged it.

Maybe a better question was, why was she attracted to him? He'd made that shocking discovery yesterday when he was struck with a powerful urge to kiss her. In that crazy moment, he'd glimpsed an answering spark in her blue eyes. She'd wanted him to kiss her. And he had no idea why.

From their very first meeting, they'd been at odds. He'd done nothing but berate or lecture her since she walked into his office in those ridiculous three-inch heels. But in spite of the yelling, he sensed she was as drawn to him as he was to her.

She'd felt the electricity flash between them as surely as he had. She also had to know that nothing could ever come of their relationship. He was her boss. She was a member of his faculty. *End of story.*

"It's going to be a first-class club," he reassured her. "They'd be foolish not to come."

She smiled up through her lashes at him. "That was sweet of you to say. You'd better be careful. That's the second nice thing you've said to me in twenty-four hours."

"I'll be on my guard."

"Can I impose on your temporary good nature for a favor before you revert to Mr. Harris, Beast-Principal?"

"You can try."

"Would you help me hang these last four posters? I had a terrible time with the ones I hung yesterday. I'm too short to place them high enough."

The request was an obvious bid for his company. They

both knew she could knock out the job in fifteen minutes with the aid of a chair and a couple of thumbtacks. If he had any sense at all, he'd tell her he was busy and she'd have to handle it alone.

"Yeah, I can do that." Evidently sense was in short supply.

"Excellent. You grab the posters. I'll get the tacks."

They walked the empty halls together, Sunni taking two steps to every one of his.

"Seems lonely without wall-to-wall kids," Sunni said. "It's kinda sad."

"I think so, too. During the summer months when I'm here by myself, I get the feeling that the building is waiting, looking forward to the day when the halls are filled with kids." He regretted the words the minute they were out of his mouth. They sounded so sappy and sentimental and. . .weird.

Sunni didn't seem to think so. "You love this place, don't you?"

He looked around. "Yeah."

"Have you always wanted to be principal?"

"No, I grew up thinking I would take my father's place at—uh, the family business," he finished quickly. "It wasn't until my senior year of high school that I discovered I wanted to be in education."

"What changed your mind?"

"I had a great teacher. Mr. Evans. He taught history. He was truly amazing. His students didn't just learn history under him; they experienced it. He was totally into teaching and his students. He felt a genuine calling from God to reach out to kids, to invest himself in them, and to influence their lives."

"And did he?"

"He influenced me. He opened my eyes to the fact that

there is more to living than profit and loss statements. He made me believe I had the power to impact the world for good."

"Mr. Evans sounds like a great man. I wonder if he's still teaching."

"Absolutely. We keep in touch through e-mails."

"I bet he's proud to know one of his students went on to become a principal."

"You'd never know it. He's a crusty old guy. Compliments aren't his style."

Sunni turned laughing eyes to him. "Crusty, huh? Does that sound like someone we know? Like mentor, like mentee?"

There it was again. That incredible urge to sweep her into his arms and kiss her. He plunged his hands into his pockets.

"Here's a good spot," she said, her attention focused on an empty wall. "Let's hang one here."

Ethan took the top poster and held it against the wall at his eye level. A cloud of glitter sprinkled down on his head. "How's this?"

Sunni backed up two steps and cocked her head to the side. "How about an inch higher?"

He slid the poster up another inch. "Better?"

"Perfect."

Instead of handing him the tacks, Sunni scooted up beside him. When she rose up on tiptoe, her arms overhead to push the thumbtack into the corner of the cardboard, she brushed against him. If that wasn't enough to drive him to distraction, his nose was mere inches from her hair that smelled of flowers. The combination of warmth and fragrance jolted through his system.

Forget professionalism. He had to kiss her.

"Sunni?" he whispered.

"Hey, Ethan! Are you moving in on my girl?"

Coach Rawley caught them by surprise. Neither had heard his sneakered approach.

Sunni was turned and facing Jerry in one graceful move. Her cheeks were flushed as she said, "Hi, Jerry. Mr. Harris and I were just hanging posters."

"I see that." His disapproving tone said he saw a whole lot more.

"I needed someone taller," she explained. "To get the posters at the right level."

"I wish you'd have asked me," Jerry grumbled. "I'd have been happy to help you."

"I, uh, didn't know you were still here. The place was so quiet I thought Mr. Harris and I were the only ones."

"I saw that, too."

Ethan cleared his throat. "Now that we know you're here, you can help us out. It won't take but a minute if we all pitch in."

They moved around the corner. Sunni assigned them each a spot to hang their poster. Ethan noted she was able to hang hers at a satisfactory level without his help or the aid of a chair.

When she turned from hanging it, he caught her eye and gave her a look that said he was wise to her tricks. She shrugged and flashed him an unrepentant wink.

"Is that all you've got?" Jerry asked.

Sunni nodded. "That's it. I appreciate your help."

"No problem. Next time, ask *me*. I'm always available."

"I'll remember that."

Jerry looked from Sunni to Ethan. "So, are you two leaving?" It was obvious he wouldn't be going anywhere until they did.

"Yeah," Ethan said. "I still have to run some papers by the district office."

"I just need to get my purse from the home ec room," Sunni said.

"We can all walk out together," Jerry decided.

With a quick shared look, Sunni and Ethan fell into step with Jerry.

ten

Sunni's stomach was tied up in knots. She'd poured herself, body and soul, into the Club. Since the idea first formed in her mind, she'd focused all her prayers and energies on making it the best club ever.

Each poster and announcement had been lovingly crafted to draw the kids to the first meeting. She'd labored over the menu of refreshments to strike a delicate balance between special treat and something cool enough to appeal to the jaded palate of a thirteen-year-old. Now that Friday afternoon had finally arrived, she feared she'd missed something—left out some critical detail.

What if nobody comes?

That terrifying thought had kept Sunni awake most of the night. These kids didn't realize an invitation to a Sunni Vanderclef party was a coveted prize. People courted her months prior to her annual spring luncheon to be assured of a place on the select guest list. But middle schoolers didn't read the society pages. They didn't know she was a hostess extraordinaire. They might think an afternoon in front of the television watching twenty-year-old game show reruns was preferable to her club.

Nerves sent a fresh wave of adrenaline crashing over her. Though she had twenty minutes until the guests were due, she couldn't sit and relax. She had to be doing something.

She walked to the kitchens to inspect the refreshments

for the hundredth time. Ramon had smuggled them to her through the back door during her free period. Now fully aware of district policies on security, thanks to the four-page memo from Ethan, she knew she ought to have had Ramon meet her at the front door after he'd been cleared by the office. But following rules would have meant a lot of extra work lugging heavy boxes of food from one end of the school to the other, so once again, Sunni opted to ignore district policy. Next time, she promised herself, she'd do it by the book.

She'd arranged the sandwiches and chips on platters on bright, checkered tablecloths spread out along the countertops of kitchen one. She'd set up a cute tin washtub on a coordinating checkered tablecloth across the aisle on the counter in kitchen two. As soon as she'd dismissed her last class, she'd filled the washtub with chilled canned sodas and poured several bags of ice over them to keep them cold.

Ramon had outdone himself. The food, enough to feed an army, looked great. Instead of the fussy finger sandwiches her usual crowd would prefer, he'd created cute little individual hoagies, sure to be a hit among young teens. And he'd brought three kinds of chips and an untold variety of sodas.

To establish a nice traffic flow, Sunni displayed the sweets in kitchen three. Two-tiered servers placed at intervals along a checkered tablecloth were loaded down with brownies, cookies, and tiny chocolate tarts.

It all looked wonderful. Now if only someone would come to appreciate it.

She glanced at the clock. Three twenty. Her nerves jumped. She wondered why she didn't hear anyone in the hall.

She slowly approached the door to the hall. She wanted to peek, but she was half afraid of what she would find.

Amanda from the sixth-period class peered in. "Hi, Miss Vanderclef. Am I too early for the Club?"

Giddy with relief, Sunni pulled her into an exuberant embrace. "Not at all. You're right on time. I'm so glad you're here."

Amanda returned the hug, her face flushed with pleasure. "I wouldn't miss it for anything. Not after you asked me specially to come."

Sunni raised her eyes heavenward in silent thanks for the impulse that led her to pull Amanda aside before class and ask her personally to join the Club. "We're going to have a great time."

Amanda's gaze took in the empty room. "Where is everybody?"

Sunni shrugged as if that nagging question wasn't giving her palpitations. "I don't know. Come in, and you can fix a plate while we wait for them to get here."

Too shy to protest, Amanda allowed Sunni to lead her to the food. She obediently placed a sandwich and a few chips on a plate, but Sunni sensed she'd be too nervous to eat in front of anyone.

The minutes ticked by. At three thirty, two skinny seventh-grade boys dragged in. Sunni raced to the door to greet them.

"Hi. I'm Sunni Vanderclef, the faculty sponsor of the Club. Who are you?"

The first boy kept his eyes trained on the floor. "I'm Seth," he mumbled.

Sunni patted his shoulder. "Welcome, Seth. And who are you?" she asked the second boy who hung back several feet.

He shrugged. "I'm Kirk. I don't want to join any clubs. I'm

just here because I carpool with Seth and my mom says she's not going to make two trips."

Charming. "I'm glad you're here, whatever the reason," Sunni said with a determined smile. "Why don't you two grab something to eat while we wait for the others?"

To make the room more conducive to relationship building, Sunni had pushed the desks into the back and placed a circle of twenty chairs in their place. Amanda sat hunched in a chair on one side of the circle, nervously balancing her plate on her lap. After Seth and Kirk had filled plates, they took two seats on the opposite side of the circle. The three of them were careful not to make eye contact.

Sunni waited at the door until three forty. The hall was empty, silent. No one else was coming. Her fervent prayers, twenty hand-lettered posters, and fifty minihoagies netted her two club members and a stranded carpool tagalong.

Having been drilled in the responsibilities of a hostess since childhood, Sunni was careful not to let any of her disappointment show.

"I guess this is everyone," she said cheerfully as she joined the others in the circle.

"Not much of a club," Kirk muttered.

Sunni ignored him. "Let's go ahead and close the circle," she instructed, borrowing an old Bible study term. "We'll push the empty chairs out and scoot our chairs closer together."

The only sound in the room was the scraping of chairs against the tile floor.

"Okay," she said once they were settled. "Let's go around the circle and introduce ourselves. Who wants to go first?"

All three pairs of eyes locked on the floor.

After an uncomfortable silence, Sunni chirped, "Why don't I

start? I'm Sunni Vanderclef. I'm the home ec teacher this year."

"You're the one who almost burned down the school," Kirk accused with glee.

"Yes, thank you," Sunni said with a tight smile. "What about you, Kirk? Would you introduce yourself and tell us a little bit about you?"

He folded his arms across his chest. "I don't see why I have to. I'm not joining."

"You are with us today," Sunni gritted out, "so you may as well participate."

"I can just sit out in the hall until you're done," he offered.

"You will sit right there and introduce yourself. Now."

He slumped in his chair. "I'm Kirk Paxton. And I'm not joining."

"Thank you, Kirk. What about you, Seth?"

Seth's chin rested on his collarbone. "I'm Seth Hall," he mumbled.

"It's great to have you, Seth. I don't know you well, but I'm going to guess you are a pretty terrific kid."

He shrugged, his eyes still on his feet.

"I'd like to suggest something to you. A way for you to show others how terrific you are. I want you to look at me."

Curious, he lifted his eyes to hers.

"Good. Now I want you to introduce yourself again, this time being careful to meet the eyes of the group. Eye contact is an important means of communication. It tells people you are open and interested. Looking people in the eye is a way to make them like you."

His gaze darted to hers, then Amanda's, then Kirk's, before heading back to the tile. "I'm Seth Hall."

Rome wasn't built in a day. Sunni reached over to pat his

hand. "Excellent." She turned to Amanda. "Last but not least, would you please introduce yourself?"

Mindful of the eye contact tip, Amanda was careful to look Sunni in the eyes. "I'm Amanda Fenton. I'm an eighth grader, and I'm very excited about the Club."

"Thank you."

Sunni had drawn up a detailed agenda for how the hour-long meeting would be spent. She planned for the introduction segment of the program to take fifteen minutes. Even with Seth introducing himself twice, the whole process took less than three minutes.

The next fifteen minutes had been allotted to mingling and eating. The boys had already devoured their sandwiches and sucked down their sodas. Poor Amanda was too self-conscious even to sip her drink. *So much for the eating.* Since the idea of their mingling was laughable, Sunni moved on.

"For our next order of business, I would like to read the mission statement for the Club, and then we'll elect officers."

"Officers?" Kirk hooted. "You've only got two members. Why do you need officers?"

Though she wondered the same thing, she wasn't about to admit it to Mr. Smarty. "Because it's an official club. Official clubs require a governing body. Besides, we are planning to grow."

"Fat chance," Kirk muttered.

Sunni read the mission statement and asked if anyone had anything they wanted to say about it. Amanda shook her head, and the boys stared at the floor so Sunni proceeded with the elections.

"Amanda and Seth, does either of you have any interest in being an officer?"

Amanda's arm shot up. "Miss Vanderclef, I'd like to be the president."

"Is that agreeable to you?" Sunni asked the top of Seth's head.

He shrugged.

"Let's put it to the vote," Sunni said. "All in favor of Amanda as president, please say *aye*."

"This is ridiculous," Kirk complained.

"Nobody asked you," Sunni said.

Amanda was the unanimous winner.

"Seth, would you like to be the secretary/treasurer of the Club?"

He lifted his face enough so that Sunni could see his eyes. "Yeah. Okay."

"Let's vote. All in favor of Seth for secretary/treasurer, please say *aye*."

He almost smiled when she announced him as the winner.

"Can we go now?" Kirk whined.

If only they could. "It's four o'clock. Your mother won't be here until four thirty."

"Then can we eat?"

"Go ahead. I need to meet with the officers about club business."

After a dramatic eye roll, Kirk loped back to the kitchens.

"Since the purpose of our club is to foster friendships, I'd like suggestions from the two of you as to what kinds of activities we should have."

"Maybe we can talk more about how to make people like us," Amanda suggested.

Sunni's heart broke a little. "I like that idea. We can line up speakers on relationship building."

Kirk was back with a full plate. "Boring."

"And maybe we could go places," Amanda said, following Sunni's lead to ignore him.

"Like where?" Sunni asked.

"The mall. . ."

"That'd be gross," Kirk said.

"Do you have any better ideas?" Amanda shot back, giving Sunni some hope for the young girl.

"Maybe we could go to movies," Seth suggested to his shoes.

The brainstorming, if you could call Amanda and Kirk's sniping at each other and Seth's study of his feet brainstorming, went on for several minutes. Sunni looked at the clock. She'd run out of agenda, and they had twenty-seven more minutes to fill.

She wanted to cry. Her inexhaustible supply of cheerfulness had run dry. She didn't want to be nice. She wanted to curl up in a ball and die.

Sunni sent up a frantic prayer. *Lord, I'm trying to keep up my end of the bargain and use my gift, but I'd welcome a little help.*

Salvation arrived in the form of Ethan Harris.

And what a form it was. He might disapprove of having money, but he didn't appear to be opposed to spending it. She didn't know what principals earned, but it must be a bundle if he could afford designer slacks and Italian loafers.

His shirt had all the earmarks of hand tailoring, and she was sure that was a several-hundred-dollar silk tie wrapped around his handsome throat.

"Hi. I'm sorry I'm late," Ethan said to the room at large. "I wanted to be here from the beginning, but I got tied up on a call. How's everything going?"

It had to be obvious that a club with three members wasn't going at all, but Sunni was so grateful for his pretense she could have kissed him.

His presence recharged her. "Very well," Sunni said with a smile. "We've just finished officer elections."

"And I'm the president," Amanda crowed.

He shook her hand. "Congratulations, Amanda. You'll do an excellent job."

He knew her name. Sunni marveled that Ethan knew the name of one shy young girl out of a school of several hundred.

"And Seth is our secretary/treasurer," Sunni said.

"Congratulations." Ethan gave him a firm handshake. He turned to Kirk. "And what are you going to do?"

"I'm going to try to talk my mom into making two trips so I don't have to come to any more lame meetings."

Ethan didn't bat an eye. "That's a shame. You could be a real asset to the Club."

"How do you figure that?" Kirk wanted to know.

Sunni wanted to know the same thing.

"You have a lot of contacts. You could help invite people to the Club."

Kirk puffed out his chest like a pigeon. Sunni doubted very much that a skinny seventh grader who smelled like week-old gym socks was a big man on campus, but it was obvious he thought of himself as one.

"Yeah," he said with a weak attempt at modesty. "I guess I do know a lot of people."

Ethan shrugged. "It's up to you."

He turned to Sunni. "What's next on the agenda, Ms. Vanderclef?"

She tried to telegraph her desperation through her eyes while keeping her voice pleasant and even. "I've run through everything I wanted to accomplish today."

Who says men have to have things spelled out? He picked up her distress signal and winked his acknowledgment.

"Since you have a few minutes until quitting time, I think we should play a round of championship Hangman. Girls against the boys."

Hangman? Sunni vaguely remembered a game involving stick drawings and filling in the blanks. *Is this cool enough for middle-school kids?*

Evidently so. Possibly because of the challenge between the sexes, the kids really got into the game. At four thirty, each team had three wins.

"I declare the match a draw," Ethan said.

Both teams seemed pleased. Sunni knew the bulk of her pleasure stemmed from the fact that the interminable meeting was finally over.

"Amanda, as president, it's your job to adjourn the meeting."

"She needs a gavel," Kirk said.

Amanda improvised and clanked her still-full soda can on the desk. "This meeting of the Club is adjourned."

Sunni and Ethan walked the kids to the front doors where their rides waited at the curb. Sunni sighed when the last car pulled away.

"So tell me about it," Ethan said in a voice so gentle and understanding it brought tears to her eyes.

"What's to tell? It was a disaster. I threw a party, and nobody came." She hated the pathetic hitch in her voice.

"Three people came."

"Only two count. Kirk was only there by default, which he

made painfully clear half a dozen times."

"Forget Kirk. You don't need him."

"I need *someone!* This isn't the way I planned it. I prayed about this. Lots of kids were supposed to come. Kids who knew how to make eye contact and small talk. I didn't expect two hopelessly mismatched shy kids."

Ethan's voice chilled. "Don't you mean misfits?"

"No!" Indignation replaced self-pity. "What a terrible thing to accuse me of. Those children aren't misfits. They are darling." She paused. "Well, Kirk is not darling, but Amanda and Seth are. But as sweet as they are, they are not enough to build a club on. I need popular kids."

"I thought you weren't trying to start a sorority."

"Is that what you think this is all about? Building a club to feed my ego?"

"I didn't until I heard you complaining that you didn't get the right kids."

Sunni took a deep breath. He wasn't the enemy. "The whole purpose of the Club is to help the kids who don't have friends find a place to fit in. I had hoped that by mingling with the popular kids they would pick up a few of the social skills they lack and that the popular kids would realize these kids are okay. Then they would include them in the popular activities."

"That's a pretty tall order."

"But not impossible. I want to do this, Ethan." She paused, aware she'd addressed him by his first name, then took a breath and continued. "You told me to find a need and fill it. Seth and Amanda and lots of other kids need friends. I'm going to help them make them."

"I believe you can do anything you put your mind to."

"That's sweet of you to say, especially since you saw me in

that meeting. I was about to lose it. You saved me. I really owe you."

Ethan shrugged. "I was glad to help out. It was fun. But I don't think you were in real danger of losing it. You'd have managed to pull it off if I hadn't been there. Give yourself some credit. You're actually pretty good with kids."

She stopped walking and turned to face him. "Do you honestly think so?"

He smiled down at her. "Cross my heart."

"That's the nicest thing anyone's ever said to me." Sunni gave him a long assessing look. "I suppose it would be a bad idea for me to kiss you? Right there"—she pointed to his face—"on your cheek."

The question startled him. He swallowed hard and cleared his throat before saying, "In my professional opinion, I think kissing a coworker is a very bad idea."

She sighed. "You're probably right. Too bad."

eleven

Jennifer and Sunni shared a table in the cafeteria. Jennifer was digging in to her mystery entrée while Sunni sipped her diet cola. "Did you hear my announcement about the Club's officer elections?"

Jennifer nodded. "Yeah. It sounded good."

"Think it fooled anybody?"

"No way. Middle schoolers are sharp. They can spot a scam a mile away." Jennifer put down her fork. "You've heard what they're calling your club, haven't you?"

"I'm afraid to ask."

"The loser club."

Her heart sank. Brutally honest friends could be a blessing or a curse. Today Sunni wished her friend weren't quite so truthful. "But why?"

"Look at the membership, Sunni. Two confirmed dweebs."

"What am I going to do to attract nondweebs?"

Jennifer thought a minute. "Your family is rich, right?"

"Yeah."

"So bribe kids to join."

❧

Jennifer might have been kidding when she told Sunni to bribe kids to join her club, but after giving the matter considerable thought, Sunni decided the idea had merit. The trick was to be subtle enough that nobody knew they were being bribed. She supposed Ethan would think she was

119

using Daddy's money to buy a club, and technically he might be right; but in this case, the end justified the means.

She decided to run the idea by him after school.

"Hi, Mrs. Leeper. Is Mr. Harris in his office?"

The older woman beamed up at her. "Hello, dear. He sure is. Would you like to speak with him?"

"Yes, ma'am, if he has a minute."

Mrs. Leeper buzzed him on the intercom to tell him Sunni was on her way in.

Ethan was standing when she walked in. He hadn't gotten around to loosening his tie yet, but he'd taken off his jacket and draped it over the back of his chair. He looked wonderful. The crisp white shirt and blue tie seemed to accentuate his broad shoulders and dark good looks. He was smiling a big white smile that displayed his perfect white teeth. A smile that said he was genuinely happy to see her. Sunni's heart lurched.

"Hello, Sunni," he said, coming around the desk toward her. He paused to sniff the air before leaning back against the corner of his desk. "To what do I owe the pleasure of this visit? I don't smell smoke."

"Very funny," she said, taking the seat directly in front of him. "I had an idea I wanted to run by you. To see what you think."

"You're looking for more professional advice."

The comment brought to mind their conversation Friday afternoon about the inadvisability of kissing coworkers. Without thinking, Sunni's gaze traveled to Ethan's cheek. As she watched, the smile faded from his lips as though he, too, remembered.

She cleared her throat and looked away. "Yes, I'm looking for advice. About my club."

"I thought your announcement this morning was very upbeat. If I didn't know better, I'd believe after one meeting that the Club was a great success."

"I didn't lie exactly," Sunni said. "I simply tried to put a positive spin on things. No point in advertising our poor turnout. That's what I wanted to talk to you about: How I can improve attendance for the next meeting."

"What's the plan?"

"I'd like to bring in a speaker, someone who could talk to the kids about makeup and hygiene. And hand out lots of giveaways."

"Giveaways? Sounds like a fancy name for a bribe."

"Nobody ever accused you of being stupid."

"Or you of being unwilling to spend Daddy's money."

"It's for a good cause," she defended.

"I agree."

Sunni opened her mouth to argue and snapped it shut when she realized what he'd said. "You do?"

He smiled at the surprise in her voice. "Absolutely. It sounds like an excellent way to attract some new members."

"So it's okay to bring someone in?"

"Sure. Just give me the names so I can have them cleared."

"Great." She stood to leave. "Thanks."

Ethan reached out and caught her arm. "Wait."

She looked up into his face. "Yes?"

"I wanted to talk to you. About Friday."

"About my telling you I wanted to kiss you?"

"Yeah."

She shook her head. "You don't need to say anything. I shouldn't have said it. It was wrong. I was being crazy—"

"You understand why we can't—"

"Sure. Totally. I mean, you're my boss. That would be too weird."

"Not to mention unprofessional."

"And crazy. You and I are so different."

"Completely."

"And even if it were possible, which it's not," Sunni rambled on, "I mean, you and I would never work out."

"Never."

"So forget I ever said it."

"Consider it forgotten."

❧

Sunni turned the knob and pushed open the library door without making a sound. Unfortunately, since the assembled group was facing her, no way could her late entrance go undetected.

"Good morning, Ms. Vanderclef," Ethan said. "Nice of you to join us. And only thirty minutes late. You're improving."

The faculty chuckled.

"Go ahead and find a seat," he said. "I think one's back there next to Jennifer."

Sunni scooted to the seat Jennifer was saving.

"I'm handing out a questionnaire I want you all to complete. With the first month under our belts, I want to get a feel for how you think things are going." Ethan went to each table distributing a stack of papers. At Sunni's table, he stopped and turned to the group. "You'll find a place at the bottom for suggestions. Please take your time in filling them out. And be honest. If you feel something needs to be changed, I want to know about it."

Sunni's hand shot up. "I have a suggestion. I think we should reverse the direction we're facing in these meetings, so if someone comes in late, they won't disturb everyone."

"I have a better suggestion. Why don't you come on time?"

"I fully intended to be here at ten o'clock, but I broke a nail." She held up her finger to show him. "I had to make an emergency appointment at the salon. That's why I'm late."

"At least it was something important like a broken nail instead of some frivolous excuse."

She pitched her voice for his ears only. "No need to be sarcastic. I was simply making a suggestion."

"Suggestion noted. Now be quiet so the others can work." The smile he flashed her took the sting out of his words.

The faculty quit pretending they weren't listening to Ethan and Sunni's conversation and settled in to work on their questionnaires.

Jennifer wrote something on a half sheet of paper and slipped it to Sunni. Sunni's eyes widened as she read, *You know how you always say Ethan doesn't like you? I think you're wrong. I'm beginning to think he likes you a lot.*

Sunni wrote back, *What makes you think so?*

Jennifer scribbled, *Something about the way he looks at you, even when he's fussing at you. I don't know how to describe it exactly, but I know I wouldn't mind if my fiancé looked at me that way.*

Sunni knew exactly how to describe the look. *Electrifying.* Nobody had ever looked at her that way before, even Mason.

It had to be unintentional. She and Ethan had agreed that nothing could ever come of them as a couple. They'd promised to forget about her comment on kissing.

Unfortunately, if his memory were anything like hers, he hadn't forgotten the question or the feelings that led up to it. She thought she'd do a whole lot better forgetting if he'd quit looking at her that way.

After giving the group ample time to finish the surveys, Ethan collected them with the promise of reading each one. Sunni didn't know how most schools operated, but she'd be willing to guess Ethan was one of a select few principals so dedicated to keeping his faculty happy. She liked that about him.

She slumped down into her chair with a sigh. She liked everything about him. Not a promising beginning for a woman pledged to forget any feelings she had for the man.

"For the next order of business, the custodian reported that the back door at the end of Hall Two had been found unlocked twice over the last month. Though he didn't see it happen, he feels that someone inside the school was using the door to allow access to unauthorized visitors."

Sunni fought the urge to squirm.

Ethan scanned the room as if looking for a random person to call on. His gaze came to rest on her. "Ms. Vanderclef, can you remind the group about district policy on admitting non-school personnel into the building?"

Coincidence? She didn't think so. She was beginning to think there was something to Ethan's remark that principals were omniscient. "Yes, Mr. Harris. According to a district ruling dating back to 1998, any person desiring entrance into a public school building must do so through the front door. They must present themselves at the main office to receive clearance before proceeding."

"Thank you, Ms. Vanderclef." To the group, he said, "I think the policies are clear. We know they are in place for the safety of our students." He allowed his gaze to rest on Sunni again. "This is the last time I expect to address this issue."

The meeting ran another forty-five minutes. Before closing,

Ethan asked for any announcements.

Sunni raised her hand. "Homeroom teachers, please don't forget to mention the Club meeting this coming Friday. You might remind them about the giveaways and door prizes."

One of the women asked, "Can teachers come?"

Sunni laughed. "No, but I promise to save any leftover giveaways for you."

❧

Sunni's first thought when she called the Club meeting to order was that she wasn't going to have any leftovers. Her heart soared. *Thank You, Lord.* The turnout for the second meeting far surpassed her expectations. Sixteen boys, not counting Kirk who assured her on his way in that he did not want to be there, and thirty-nine girls.

Sunni was pretty sure it was the promise of free makeup samples that brought them, but she didn't care. Maybe if they had a good time, they'd come back.

Because time was limited, Sunni divided the group into boys and girls. For the boys' speaker, she'd pressured Gary Oldan, an old college friend, to come and talk to them about basic hygiene under the guise of man-to-man tips. Once the guys heard how funny Gary was, they'd be putty in his hands.

For the girls' speaker, Sunni headed to the most popular cosmetic counter at the biggest department store in town and made them a deal. In return for buying a stupefying quantity of makeup to be distributed as giveaways and the promise of future sales, they would send her four or five of their makeup artists to give tips and makeovers to the girls.

Five young women in their mid-twenties garbed in pristine white smocks and toting lighted makeup mirrors and boxes of supplies arrived at the home ec room thirty minutes before the meeting. Sunni positioned them in stations around the room with the intention of dividing up the girls and distributing them evenly. She had to run for extra chairs to accommodate the overflow crowd, but it was a labor of love. Once the meeting was underway, Sunni circulated around the room to assure all was running smoothly. As she anticipated, the boys loved Gary and gave him their undivided attention.

She was even more pleased with the girls. Within their groups of eight, they chattered like best friends. Nothing like lip gloss and eye liner to break the ice. She was especially delighted to see Amanda in the makeover chair. Sunni was certain she could feel the happiness radiating from Amanda as the artist made her up.

After a final pass to ascertain that all was well, Sunni went to work redistributing the goodies in the goody bags. Not knowing how many people to expect, she'd prepared a dozen bags for the boys and two dozen for the girls. Because of her capacity crowd, she needed to pull a few items from each bag to create more bags.

Ethan appeared at her side. "Wow! Look at this crowd. Who says money can't buy love?"

"Shh!" Sunni pressed a finger to her lips. "Somebody will hear you."

"I doubt it. They look engrossed." Ethan glanced around. "Too bad they don't pay attention like this in class."

"They would if the teachers would incorporate makeup tips in their lesson plans."

Ethan laughed. "What are you doing?"

"Stretching the booty. Sit down, and you can help me. I'm taking a few things out of each bag to create a total of seventeen bags for the boys and thirty-nine for the girls."

"What all do you have in here?" Ethan asked, peering into one of the small white paper sacks marked for boys. "Deodorant, soap, some kind of face stuff, toothpaste—Sunni, these are full-size products. I know I'll probably regret asking, but what did all this loot set you back?"

She smiled at his concern. "You don't want to know."

He shook his head. "I'm sure I don't. You know, you could always decide to collect dues."

"To pay for all this stuff, the dues would have to be the same as a country club membership with full greens privileges."

He looked at her. "Is it worth it?"

"Are you kidding? Look at Amanda. She's glowing. And look at all the girls talking to her."

"She looks pumped."

"And look at Seth. He's laughing. Earlier I actually saw him look up from the floor to answer a question." Tears filled her eyes. "My money and I are making a difference."

The hour-long meeting flew by. In no time, a tastefully made-up Amanda dismissed the meeting. It was another half hour before the chattering group cleared out.

One of the makeup artists stopped by Sunni to say, "The girls told me they have a Christmas dance coming up. If you want to work out something, I'd be happy to bring in a team to do makeup for them."

Sunni took her business card. "Thank you. I'll be in touch."

Ethan waited with Sunni until everyone had gone. He helped her put the desks back in place and carry the extra chairs to the rooms from where she'd borrowed them.

"I didn't know middle schools had dances," Sunni said.

"Just one. The Christmas dance. We have it every year."

"What's it like?"

"Painful. Nobody knows how to dance, and they're too embarrassed to try, so boys stand on one side of the gym and girls on the other."

"Sounds awful."

"And that's the good part. The bad part is chasing after couples who scatter to dark corners to neck."

"Do the teachers chaperone?" Sunni wanted to know.

"Why? Are you volunteering for a dark corner?"

It was on the tip of her tongue to say yes, if he'd promise to work the same corner. Instead, she said, "I'd like to help out."

"The home ec class usually provides the refreshments. Maybe Ramon can whip up something."

"Are you kidding? This is a great opportunity for the kids to do some cooking."

"I don't want you to be too hasty—"

"You don't think we can do it."

"It's not that. It's just—"

"It's that pesky fire alarm business," Sunni said with a martyred sigh. "No one will let me live down that one small mistake."

"Sure we will. But give me an hour or two's notice before you fire up the ovens. I want to know the fire department is at one hundred percent manpower."

twelve

By mid-November, Central Middle School was running at full throttle. The second grading period report cards had gone out, and according to the percentages, student performance was up two-tenths of a point over the numbers from the previous year.

Central's football team finished a winning season at seven and two with no major injuries. The cafeteria ladies had revamped the menu, adding chopped celery to the tossed salads and baked potatoes as a side dish option on odd-numbered Fridays.

Student and faculty morale was at an all-time high, as was PTA membership. Central Middle School was moving steadily toward another Blue Ribbon designation.

And Ethan Harris was in trouble.

He'd suspected it for some time, but his pre-Thanksgiving meeting with the district superintendent and area principals confirmed it. After listening to status reports, the superintendent asked Ethan to give his prognosis for the upcoming semester. Caught in mid-daydream, Ethan said the first thing that popped into his head. "Sunni."

That's when he knew he was in trouble. *Deep trouble.*

He wasn't in love with her. He couldn't be in love with her. But he was definitely hung up on her. If he were honest with himself, he'd admit he'd been interested in Sunni from the first time they'd met. Aggravated, but interested. Over the three months he'd known her, the interest had grown to fascination.

His initial impression of her hadn't been entirely wrong. Sunni Vanderclef *was* a rich, spoiled socialite. But she was so much more.

Her lovely frame housed a generous, godly spirit unlike anything he'd ever known. She gave freely of her time and resources without keeping an accounting. As far as he knew, she told no one what it took to build her club. The countless dollars and hours remained her secret.

Sunni didn't do things for show. She did them for love.

Beneath the expensive suits beat a heart so tender that one lonely child could wound it.

At first, he suspected the Club was nothing more than a ruse. That she was trying to parlay her one, negligible talent into a bid to finish out the school year.

Had he ever believed she had no talent? What an idiot he had been. Sunni had more talent in her pinky than he had in his whole body. Sunni's talent was joy. A kind word, a short note, or a wide smile from her spread the joy like a virus. All of Central Middle School had been infected.

Everybody loved her. The teachers loved her for the silly notes and chocolates they found in their mailboxes once a week. The students loved her because of the sense of adventure that surrounded her. She might conduct her class standing on top of her stool; she might burn the building to the ground—who knew?

Ethan loved her because—no, Ethan was determined not to love her.

Sunni was always on his mind. He thought about her when he woke up in the morning. Knowing he would see her made it worth getting out of bed. His thoughts returned to her a hundred times during the day. When something funny happened, he tried to imagine her reaction. During serious or sad moments, he wondered how he might cushion the blow for her.

Nights were the hardest. Late in the evening when he tried to clear his mind for sleep, Sunni was there, filling his thoughts, invading his dreams.

Knowing she was not immune to him somehow made it all worse. Sunni wasn't just an attractive woman; she was a teacher. One of his teachers. Any sort of relationship outside professional boundaries of boss to subordinate was strictly forbidden. The district didn't just have policies on appropriate employee relationships; they had whole manuals dedicated to the topic.

Sunni was off limits.

He reminded himself constantly. When his feet took a subconscious detour toward the home ec room, he forced himself to hurry by without stopping. The few times his self-control was particularly potent, he managed to pass by without peeking inside for a glimpse of her.

When he ran into her around the school, he made it a point to keep his greetings short and impersonal. He couldn't count the number of times he had to drag himself away before he gave into temptation and touched her. To follow through would be to risk not only his credibility but also his job.

❧

"Mr. Harris, you have a call on line three. It's your mother."

Ethan put the receiver to his ear and kicked back in his chair. "Hi, Mom. What's up?"

"I'm trying to make seating arrangements for Thanksgiving dinner."

"Great. Put me down for a seat close to the stuffing and as far from Dad as possible."

"Be nice."

"Okay, put me down for a seat close to the stuffing and at least out of shouting range of Dad."

"He's not likely to shout at you over the Thanksgiving dinner."

"No, he'll wait until dessert."

"Ethan, be fair. I think your father has been doing much better lately. You must admit it was a bit of a disappointment for him that his son didn't want to take over the family business."

"What's to take over? Dad's in excellent health. I can't see him stepping down for another twenty years."

"I know. But he's always dreamed of you working by his side."

"We've been through this before."

"You're right. I'm sorry. So how many can I put you down for?"

"One."

"Just one? You don't want to bring Chloe?"

"Who?"

"Oh dear, her mother was right. She said Chloe thought you were very distracted."

"Do I know a Chloe?"

"Ethan, dear, Chloe was the young woman you took to the board dinner three weeks ago."

"Oh yeah, the blind date."

"You don't have to say it like that. Chloe is a lovely girl, from an excellent family. You two are perfect for each other."

"Don't go there, Mom. I'm thirty years old. I don't need you to play matchmaker for me."

"If you are doing so well without me, then tell me why you are thirty years old and still single."

"I'm really involved with school."

"That's an admirable sentiment for a principal, I'm sure, but a school makes a very poor partner. You need to find someone and settle down. If Chloe didn't interest you, then I'll find someone else."

"No! I've found someone—I mean, I don't want to talk about it."

"Ethan! Why didn't you tell me?"

"It's nothing. Forget I said it."

"Humor me. Tell me about the nothing."

"She's a teacher here. Home ec."

"How awful."

Ethan laughed. "How can you say that? I haven't told you anything about her."

"You don't have to. I remember my home ec teacher from my school days. Long, stringy hair, shapeless dresses in earth tones, and dreadful flat shoes."

"That doesn't sound like this woman at all. Her hair is shoulder length, and if the blond streaks are natural, I'm a monkey. And she has a wardrobe that rivals yours."

"A home ec teacher who dresses well? I'm intrigued. Who is this marvel?"

"Nobody you would know."

"Try me."

"Uh-uh. No way."

"Shame on you, Ethan. You sound as if you don't trust me."

"I don't. Besides, ours is a professional relationship. Strictly business."

"I see. Tell me, dear—are principals allowed to fall for their business associates?"

"Absolutely not."

thirteen

"Sunni? Where have you been?" her mother demanded over the phone. "I've been calling for two hours. I was just about to drive up to that school to find out if you'd been attacked."

"Today was Club meeting. We moved it to Wednesday because of the Thanksgiving break."

"I hope you haven't exhausted yourself," her mother scolded. "I have a houseful of people coming for Thanksgiving. I'm counting on your help to entertain them."

"I'll be there."

"Good. And you'll want to look your best. Someone is coming whom you'll want to impress."

Ethan's face flashed through Sunni's mind. "Who?"

"Mason."

"I'm finished impressing Mason, Mom. He has a fiancée, remember?"

"Had a fiancée. They broke up. I knew it wouldn't last. He's been in love with you for years."

"He has a funny way of showing it, asking someone else to marry him."

"That was certainly tacky of him, but it's old news. Mason is a free man, and he's called me, hinting around for an invitation to Thanksgiving dinner."

"I'll be there, but not for Mason's sake."

"That a girl. You make him suffer a little before taking him back."

135

Sunni didn't know what she expected to feel, seeing Mason available again, but she hadn't expected the case of mild disinterest that settled over her when he took his place at her side during dinner. Could her feelings for him, feelings she thought would last a lifetime, have withered away and died in four short months? She was ashamed to admit she'd never really prayed about their relationship. She'd just assumed that since she'd met him at church he was the one for her. For the first time, she wondered if what she felt for Mason wasn't love at all but a comfortable assurance he would marry her.

After dinner he asked her to take a walk with him so they could talk. He reached out to take her hand as they strolled.

"I've missed you, Sunni."

She'd have given up her credit cards to hear those words in September. "I would have thought being engaged would have kept you busy."

"Aww, Sunni. I'm sorry. I know I've been stupid, but you have to believe me when I say I've always loved you."

Her brows shot up. "I bet that was awkward. Being in love with me and engaged to Ashley."

He gave her hand a squeeze. "You're angry. I don't blame you. I treated you badly."

She shook her head. "I should be angry, but I'm not. You did me the biggest favor of my life when you broke up with me."

"How do you figure that?"

"I always thought we would be married. Being your wife was the sum total of my aspirations. When you dumped me for Ashley, I took the teaching job at the middle school just to prove to you I am every bit as committed as Ashley."

"You don't have to prove anything to me."

"I know that now, but by taking the job, I've proved something to myself. I've proved I can make a difference."

"So you like your job."

"I love it. The teaching is okay, but the kids are the best part. They are so amazing, and in some small way, they need me."

"I need you, too."

She looked at him long and hard, this man she'd planned to spend the rest of her life with. "I don't think so, Mason. We all need somebody, I suppose, but I'm not your somebody."

"Is there someone else?"

She thought of Ethan. "I hope so. I really hope so."

❧

The long weekend was torture. Sunni thought of Ethan every moment. Not that this was anything new. Since the day they'd met, he'd never been far from her thoughts. Ethan was the kind of man who demanded an emotional response. His faculty and students adored him, his superiors admired him, and Sunni—?

Sunni wasn't sure what it was she felt for Ethan.

Professionally she admired and respected him. Even when he was avoiding her as he had over the last month, Ethan was a terrific boss. He cared about his teachers. He held them to high standards, the same ones he modeled in his own life. It was hard not to respect a man who lived out his convictions.

Her personal feelings weren't so clear.

Sunni knew she liked Ethan. He was a godly man, fun, considerate, and fabulous looking. What was not to like?

She knew she was attracted to him. Despite her promise to forget about kissing him, she'd spent long moments imagining what it would be like.

She liked, admired, and was attracted to Ethan. *Hmm.*

That sounded an awful lot like love.

She might as well admit it. She was head over heels in love with him.

Sunni didn't know what Ethan's feelings were for her. She thought he was attracted to her, but that wasn't enough for building a relationship. Lasting love required many things, not the least of which were mutual respect and admiration.

She knew she had a lot of strikes against her in the respect and admiration department.

She couldn't cook, and she couldn't sew. Could a principal respect a teacher without the most basic skills? Could he admire a teacher who didn't have one salable idea for the craft fair?

Then there was the money thing. Her family was rich. Ethan believed wealthy people were worthless and self-absorbed. Not a particularly good foundation for a loving relationship.

Though they were both Christians, their backgrounds were obviously different. While she didn't know the specifics, she had to believe that a man who hated rich people in principle must have come from the other side of the tracks. Could they overcome his social prejudices? Did he care enough to try?

Finally there was the professional thing. He was her boss. She didn't have a problem with interoffice relationships, but it was clear he did.

Four long days gave Sunni plenty of time to debate and dissect every part of their relationship. She was determined to trust God and wait on His timing, but she'd feel a whole lot better if she could talk to Ethan. She arrived at school Monday morning at six forty-five.

"Good morning, Mrs. Leeper."

"Good morning, Sunni. You're here bright and early this morning."

"I was hoping to catch Mr. Harris before he got busy."

"I'm sorry, dear. He had a district breakfast meeting. I don't expect him back before nine."

Sunni's smile slipped a few notches. "Okay. I'll try back later."

Her last student was barely out the door when Sunni flipped off the lights and sprinted to Ethan's office. She promised herself she'd play it cool. By employing subtle questions, she would discover what feelings, if any, he had for her.

Mrs. Leeper looked up as Sunni exploded through the door. "Hi, Sunni," she called as Sunni dashed by her desk. "Shall I tell Mr. Harris—?"

Too late. Sunni had already pushed open Ethan's door and closed it behind her.

Startled, he looked up from his computer screen. "Oh, hi, Sunni—"

"Did you miss me?"

He leaned back against his chair and scrunched his handsome face in confusion. "What?"

She advanced, slapping her palms on his desk. "Did you miss me? Did you think about me at all over the Thanksgiving holiday?"

He scrubbed his hands across his face. "Sunni—"

The look of misery on his face said it all. Sunni dropped into the chair across the desk from him. "You didn't, did you?"

He stared at his hands on the desk, then lifted his gaze to hers. "I think about you all the time."

She'd have felt better about the lovely compliment if it had been accompanied by a corresponding smile. He looked and sounded miserable. "Is that so wrong?" she asked.

He was silent as he stood and walked around his desk. He came to stand directly in front of her and looked straight into her eyes. "It's a problem. You work for me."

"And that's the only reason it's a problem?" she repeated for clarification. "Because of the boss-employee thing?"

"It's enough, Sunni. You drive me crazy."

"I drive you crazy?" It wasn't a declaration of love, but it sounded good all the same. She was out of her seat and on her tiptoes, her arms around his neck, in a heartbeat. "So what are you going to do about it?"

His arms closed around her waist. "I'm afraid I'm going to kiss you."

She melted against him. "Please do."

"Oh, Sunni," he whispered before placing his mouth over hers. He kissed her gently. Then, steadying her with his hands on her shoulders, he stepped back. "I'm sorry. I can't do this."

"But—"

"We are professionals, Sunni. You work for me. I can't let my personal life interfere with the job I was called to do."

fourteen

The last week of school before Christmas was a tough one. The wonder of the holidays filled the air and cut normally short attention spans in half. Teachers and students struggled to keep on task as both counted the hours until the coming break.

Sunni was especially excited. The holidays were partially responsible, but it was her burgeoning relationship with Ethan that brought the extra measure of joy to her world.

There had been no more kissing. Ethan had been adamant that principals do not kiss their teachers, so they kept things professional between them. But since being professional didn't mean they couldn't be friends, Sunni and Ethan spent as much time together as they could manage.

She loved him, no doubt about it. This was not a crush or an excess of hormones. What she felt for him was the real thing, the happily-ever-after kind of love.

She loved the sight and sound of him. She loved the way he thought and talked and lived. Ethan Harris was everything she could ever want in a man, the sum total of every spoken and unspoken desire.

She loved him so much she ached with the sheer power of it. Love filled her to overflowing. She wanted to shout it to the world.

And she couldn't tell a soul.

Though he hadn't expressly forbidden her to speak of their

relationship, Sunni knew Ethan wanted to keep it a secret. He felt that public disclosure would damage them both professionally. He was probably right, but it didn't make the secret any easier to keep.

Since their relationship was limited to late-night phone calls and an occasional meeting in his office after the last class, Sunni couldn't introduce him into her life outside school. She attended her endless whirl of holiday parties alone. Lately the parties seemed flat, no doubt because she couldn't share the experiences with the man she loved.

Hiding their relationship at school was doubly hard. One wink gone awry, one glance intercepted could spill the beans. So she had to be careful to ignore him. When he passed her in the halls, she feigned indifference though the sight of him sent her heart into palpitations. When they spoke, she limited her answers to two or three words though she wanted to pour out her heart.

Leading a double life is the pits.

But she loved Ethan. She loved him with every ounce of her being. She wanted to tell him.

She wished she could march right up to him, cup his precious face in her hands, and say, "I love you, Ethan." But she didn't dare.

They hadn't had their state-of-the-relationship discussion, the one in which both parties tell how much the other means to them. She knew she was probably rushing things, but she was ready to talk. It hadn't taken her long to know Ethan was the one, but she needed to make allowances in case his heart moved slower.

It wasn't that they hadn't had meaningful discussions. They talked about everything. Over the past few weeks, they'd shared their faith and their dreams and their fears, their favorite foods and places, even their memories. She felt she knew everything about Ethan. Except how he felt about her.

She hoped he loved her, that she filled his heart as he did hers, but he'd never said so. And she was afraid to make assumptions. After three years, she thought she'd known everything about Mason, and her assumptions had proved dead wrong. She wasn't going to make that mistake again.

So she waited. Maybe it was the holiday emphasis on love and goodwill, but Sunni was suddenly tired of being patient. She wanted to know where they stood. Patience was getting her nowhere. *Time to get some answers.* And today was a good place to start.

She caught him in his office after school.

"Hi, Sunni." He flashed her a smile that drove the temperature in the room up ten degrees. "How's it going?"

"Okay, I guess." She took a seat across from him. "The kids are animals. They are so full of holiday cheer that there's no interesting them in kitchen and food sanitation."

"Santa over sanitation? Go figure."

She chuckled. "I can't blame them. I'm pretty excited about Christmas, too."

"Big plans?"

"The usual parties and family things. What about you? What have you decided to do for the holidays?"

"I'm going to run down to Austin to spend a couple of days with the family."

She tried for a casual tone of voice. "Have you mentioned me to them?"

He cleared his throat. "Told my family about you? No, not really. Nothing specific."

"I see."

Ethan frowned. "No, I don't think you do. It's not that I haven't wanted to tell them. It's just. . ."

She waited for him to stop sputtering and explain what it was that prevented him from telling his family about her. When the sputtering lapsed into uncomfortable silence, she knew she had her answer. While she was looking for long range, Ethan was satisfied with day to day. That didn't sound like love. It seemed to Sunni that a man in love would want to share his good news with his nearest and dearest.

Was it the employer-employee thing that held him back? Maybe he was still trying to come to terms with the issue of her family's money. Or maybe he couldn't get enthusiastic about the prospect of spending the rest of his life with a home ec teacher who lacked even the most basic understanding of homemaking. Maybe he just saw her as a friend.

Sunni refused to despair. He didn't love her yet, but that didn't mean he never would. *Isn't Christmas the season for miracles?*

❧

Ethan fell back against his chair and rubbed his hands over his face. He couldn't go on like this.

He must be out of his mind to treat the woman he loved this way. Sunni was a prize to be cherished, not a dirty secret. He needed her, wanted her more than anything in his entire life. She'd become such an important part of his day that he literally ached when they weren't together.

So what was he going to do about it?

He'd been raised to be a man of integrity. His personal creed was to work hard and shoot straight. Lying was not an option.

He was reminded of the old saying that confession was good for the soul. Maybe it was time to come clean. To announce to the world that he was madly in love with the home ec teacher in his employ. And watch the sky fall in.

The minute the word leaked out that Ethan was romantically involved with an employee, the district would be all over him. The rules for employee relationships were crystal clear. The fact that he was the youngest principal in the district and an acknowledged Christian meant he was subject to closer scrutiny and responsible to maintain higher standards than his peers. Ethan had known and accepted that fact.

Since he first realized, years ago, that he wanted to become principal, he'd poured his life into making the dream a reality. No price was too high, no sacrifice too great. And when he made principal years ahead of schedule, he continued to pour himself into the position. He gave the job everything he had. God had called him to this. He wanted to be the best.

He wanted to make a difference.

He'd molded Central Middle School into a top-notch institution. One man couldn't do it alone; he owed much to his faculty. But ultimately it was his God-ordained leadership that drove Central to excellence. As principal, he was making a difference.

Could he give it all up?

"Mr. Harris, you have a call on line one. It's Kristen Hobart."

Ethan picked up the receiver, his thoughts still focused on his meeting with Sunni. "Hey, Kristen. What's up?"

"Physical therapy, physical therapy, physical therapy."

"Sounds rough."

She groaned. "They're killing me. I feel like I'm in training for a triathlon. So how is it with you? How's the menace?"

"Who?"

"The menace. My replacement. You know, the teacher who's going to be the death of you."

"Oh, you mean Sunni," Ethan said with a laugh. He thought about his current dilemma of trying to choose between the woman and the job he loved. "Nothing's changed. She's still going to be the death of me."

"I wish I could help. If only I could get the doctor to release me to come back to work."

He thought about that a moment. If Kristen returned to work as the home ec teacher, Sunni wouldn't be working for him. If Sunni weren't working for him, they would have no obstacles to their relationship. He could marry her and have her all to himself. 24/7. He was so wrapped up in his thoughts that he didn't realize he spoke them aloud. "If only you could come back."

Mrs. Leeper came across the intercom. "Mr. Harris, I'm sorry to bother you, but you have a call waiting on line two. It's your mother."

"Kristen, I have a call waiting."

"No problem. Hey, I almost forgot to tell you. I'm planning to come to the Christmas dance on Friday."

"Excellent. See you there."

Ethan clicked off line one and clicked on line two. "Hi, Mom."

"What's the matter? You sound unhappy."

"Not unhappy. I just have a lot on my mind."

"Problems with your well-dressed home ec teacher? What did you say her name was?"

"I didn't say. Nice try, though."

She huffed out a noisy breath. "Ethan, I think it's awful to refuse to tell your own mother her name. I spent fifteen long hours in labor for you."

"Fifteen? I thought it was thirteen."

"Whatever. It was a long time. I think it entitles me to know the name of the woman you love."

"I never said I loved her."

"Do you?"

"Well, yeah, but—"

"Then I should know her name. If she's important to you, she's important to me."

"I don't want you meddling."

"Meddle? Me? Honestly, Son, I don't know where you come up with these things. As if I could meddle even if I wanted to. We're half a state away."

"I'm sorry. I guess I'm paranoid lately. Her name is Sunni Vanderclef."

"Vanderclef? As in the Dallas Vanderclefs?"

"Those are the ones."

"I knew Malcolm Vanderclef. In fact, I went to school with his wife." She paused. "What is a Vanderclef doing teaching? She certainly doesn't need the money."

"I think she wants her life to count for something more than parties and shopping."

"Oh no, another activist. I thought God broke the mold after He made you. She sounds like the perfect partner for you."

"She is perfect."

"Have you made any plans? Shall I reserve the church?"

"I thought you weren't going to meddle." Ethan chuckled. "No plans yet. We still have some things to work out."

"I'm sure you can handle it."

"I can. Without any help from your meddling."

"I know you have a lot on your mind so I won't take offense that you've called me a meddler twice in the same conversation."

"Thanks. So what did you call for?"

"Nothing special. Just wanted to see how you were. Mothers do that sort of thing. Anyway I have some calls to make so I'll let you get back to work."

Ethan hung up the receiver and sighed. It wasn't true. He couldn't handle it. He'd studied the situation from every angle but couldn't find a solution.

How could he keep the woman and the job he loved?

"Father, I'm desperate. I want to do the job You've called me to, but I want Sunni in my life, too. Is it selfish to want them both? Show me Your way and give me the courage to walk in it."

fifteen

The home ec room had been divided into twelve stations—six for hair, six for makeup. Sunni had invited the female members of the Club to come by after school on Friday and get a special hairstyle or makeup for the Christmas dance that night. The services were free and available on a first-come, first-serve basis.

This time Sunni didn't foot the bill. The stylists came courtesy of one of the eighth-grade mothers who owned a salon. She was so pleased with the effects of the Club on her son that she volunteered to bring a crew up to the school to help the girls get ready for the big dance.

Likewise, the makeup specialists came gratis. They enjoyed their first visit to the school so much they convinced the store management to send them back.

Sunni was so touched by the generosity of these busy women that she cried. They were using their God-given skills to serve. She made a point to get to each station with a hug and a personal word of thanks for the volunteers before the girls arrived.

By four o'clock, the room was a hive of activity. Since Sunni had the responsibility for overseeing the dance refreshments and decorations in the gym, she asked Jennifer and several moms to maintain order in the home ec room.

Excitement about the biggest social event of the year combined with euphoria that school was out until January made for a festive atmosphere. It was like a party before the party. The munchies and drinks Ramon sent capped off the party spirit.

"You sure know how to throw a party," Jennifer said before popping a canapé in her mouth.

Sunni smiled at the chaos. "The girls are really having a good time, aren't they?"

"Are you kidding? This is every little girl's dream come true. Mine, too. I'm hoping one of the makeup artists can squeeze me in."

Sunni laughed. "I'm sure they'd be happy to."

"What about you? Are you going to get made up?"

Sunni shook her head. "No time. I'll be lucky to change clothes."

"You're going to want to look your best. Rumor is that the paragon is coming to the dance tonight."

"The who?"

"Kristen Hobart, the ex-home ec teacher. I heard she told Ethan she was coming tonight."

"On a stretcher?"

Jennifer laughed. "No, goofy. On her legs. The accident was five months ago. I imagine she's pretty much healed up by now."

"I've heard so much about her that I'm looking forward to finally meeting her."

Assured that everything was running smoothly in make-over central, Sunni crossed the hall to the gym where Coach Jerry was supervising the hanging of streamers and balloons. When he saw her approaching, he climbed down off the ladder and hurried to her side.

"How's it look?"

Red and silver streamers were strung from the basketball goals to the center of the ceiling, creating a canopy effect. Strings of tiny white lights were interwoven to add a touch of awe. "It's wonderful. Jerry, you've done a terrific job."

He flashed her a big smile. "I'm glad you like it. And look what I brought to spice things up." He lifted a mistletoe ball for her inspection.

She shook her head. "These are junior high students, Jerry. They don't need spice. They need cold showers."

His smile crumpled. "You don't want me to hang it?"

She smiled and patted his arm to soften the blow. "Absolutely not. The chaperones will have their hands full as it is."

"I hate for it to go to waste." He dangled it over their heads and wiggled his eyebrows at her. "What do you say we try it out?"

Sunni rolled her eyes. "Honestly, Jerry, do you ever think of anything else?"

"Sure. Football."

Kirk walked over to them, carrying a platter stacked high with brownies. "Miss Vanderclef, where do you want these?"

"That was nice of your mother to send food," Sunni said. "I didn't think you'd be coming to the dance."

He struck a pose reminiscent of John Travolta in *Saturday Night Fever*. "Sure I'm coming. I've got to show off my moves."

Sunni laughed. "I can't wait to see them. Come on. Let me show you where we've set up for refreshments."

Sunni led Kirk to the far wall where she'd arranged eight long tables for refreshments. The shimmery silver tablecloths she'd borrowed from the country club transformed the scarred tables from middle-school grunge to holiday dazzle. The Club president's mother was arranging the food as people dropped it off. Kirk handed over the brownies and disappeared.

Sunni surveyed the tables. "Mrs. Fenton, this looks lovely. You have a real knack for making everything look appetizing."

"Do you think so? I haven't had to do much. Everyone has sent such delicious stuff that all I've had to do is find a place for it on the table."

"I appreciate your help."

Mrs. Fenton smiled. "It's my pleasure. To be honest, I've been looking for a way to repay even a small amount of what you've done for my Amanda."

"She's a sweetie."

"Yes, she is, but nobody appreciated her until she joined your club. She's a different girl—so confident and happy. Do you know I have to limit the amount of time she talks on the phone every night just so the rest of the family can use it?"

Sunni laughed. "I'm so glad she's made some friends."

"She learned how to make friends from listening to you. You probably don't know it, but you're her idol."

Sunni felt her face heat with the high praise. "Thank you. I'm not sure I'm worthy of such an honor, but I'm grateful."

Mrs. Fenton waved her hands over the food. "Most of the people who contributed food have told me they wanted to do something nice for you because of all you've done for their kids. You're a very special woman, and we're lucky to have you."

For the rest of the afternoon, Sunni floated a good two feet off the floor on the strength of Mrs. Fenton's words. The parents thought she was special. They thought they were lucky to have her.

When Ethan had challenged Sunni to do something for

the kids, she'd had no idea how much blessing would come back to her.

She watched for Ethan so she could share her discovery with him, but he never showed up for the predance preparations. Jerry mentioned seeing the district superintendent in Ethan's office so perhaps he was in a meeting. *No matter.* She'd catch him tonight to tell him of her epiphany.

Sunni had a little over an hour to go home and change before it was time to get back up to school. Ethan had plenty of parent chaperones for the dance, but he wanted all his teachers to make an appearance if possible.

She wanted to make an especially good appearance tonight. She and Jennifer may have joked about it, but the truth was, Sunni was a bit nervous about Kristen Hobart. She hadn't forgotten Jennifer's suspicion that Kristen was "on the catch" for Ethan. She had no intention of letting some overachieving woman steal her man. Since Ethan didn't appear to be convinced he was in love with Sunni, he might be susceptible to the wiles of another woman.

For tonight, she needed simple elegance and drop-dead gorgeous. She selected a knee-length dress of forest green velvet. A simple platinum necklace and earrings and a terrific new pair of shoes completed the look.

She turned this way and that in front of her full-length mirror to study the results. She smiled. "Take that, Kristen Hobart."

⋅❧⋅

Sunni followed the crowd through the front doors and down the hall to the gym. She thought her hand-lettered placards on easels welcoming guests to the Christmas dance and directing them to the gym were a nice touch. Excellence was in the details.

She paused for a moment at the open doors to the gym to get the full effect. The DJ had already cranked up the music. Overhead, the strings of lights twinkled. Beneath the glittering canopy, kids dressed in their Sunday best boogied to some trendy boy band. Volunteer moms and dads chatted as they served at the refreshment tables. Around the perimeter of the gym, kids talked or watched the dancers. Teachers and chaperones seemed to be everywhere, laughing and talking.

Sunni smiled. The Christmas "Night of Miracles" dance was a success.

She'd only taken a step or two into the room when Ethan found her. She had the impression he'd been waiting for her. He wore a dark suit, white shirt, and tie with little red Santas on it. He looked impossibly handsome. And troubled.

Sunni placed a hand on his arm. "Ethan, what's the matter?"

"Nothing."

She frowned up at him. "It doesn't look like nothing."

He smiled then. "I want us to talk, after things settle down in here."

Sunni's heart leaped. He wanted to talk. It could only mean one thing: Ethan was initiating their state-of-the-relationship discussion.

"Sure," Sunni said with an answering smile. "Just find me when you're ready."

He winked before disappearing into the crowd.

The music and lights and bustle around her blurred to a pleasant din as Sunni stood rooted to the spot. Ethan loved her. She'd gotten her holiday miracle.

"Hey, girl, what are you doing standing there, staring off into space? Don't you want to see Kristen?"

At the touch of Jennifer's hand, Sunni came back to earth. "Hi, Jennifer. I'm just absorbing a little of the party atmosphere."

"Is that what you call it? Looked like daydreaming to me."

"I guess I was." Sunni focused on her friend. "You look beautiful."

"Thanks. You, too."

"So where is Ms. Home Ec?"

"Over there by the refreshments table. The tall woman in the red dress with her back to us. She was hanging on Ethan a little while ago, but it looks as if he made his escape."

The two of them started making their way through the crowd toward the refreshments. Sunni studied her quarry as they inched along. Good profile, nice posture. Terrible dress. What would possess a woman to wear anything with row after row of ruffles? Poor thing looked like a flamenco dancer. Or a red wedding cake.

Aloud Sunni said, "She's prettier than I expected."

"She does look good tonight," Jennifer agreed, "if you can get past the dress. But don't worry," she added loyally. "She doesn't hold a candle to you."

If she'd been worried earlier, she wasn't now. Kristen may have been hanging on Ethan, but it was Sunni he wanted to talk to. "Come on," Sunni said as they closed in. "Introduce us."

Kristen was talking to several parents. Rather than interrupt their conversation, Sunni and Jennifer hung back to wait their turn.

"The dance turned out really nice," Kristen was saying in a carrying voice. "I'm shocked. After everything Ethan's told me about my temporary replacement, I thought she'd make a mess of it."

Sunni grabbed Jennifer's arm when her friend took a step toward Kristen with a martial light in her eyes. "Wait."

Jennifer tried to shake off Sunni's hand. "No way. She can't talk that way about you."

"Are you saying Mr. Harris doesn't like Ms. Vanderclef?" one of the parents was asking.

"Well, you didn't hear it from me, but he calls her *the menace*. And when I talked to him the other day, he practically begged me to come back."

"Don't listen," Jennifer hissed in Sunni's ear. "Ethan would never say anything like that about you."

But he had. He'd told Sunni to her face he thought she was a menace. It was unlikely a coincidence that Kristen would come up with the same unflattering nickname.

Sunni felt sick. And stupid. She thought Ethan wanted to talk state-of-the-relationship. More likely he wanted to talk state-of-employment. As in termination.

"I have to go." Sunni turned on her heel, her only thought, *escape*.

Jennifer was right behind her. "No. Wait, Sunni. Kristen's crazy. She doesn't know what she's talking about. It's obvious she's jealous. Look at this party—it's fantastic. She's mad because you did something better than she could do."

Sunni's mind raced as she threaded her way through the crowd. Jennifer could be right. Kristen might be speaking out of spite. Or jealousy could have provoked her to divulge hers and Ethan's plans before he had time to break them to Sunni.

Sunni had known from the beginning that her teaching contract was a temporary one. The day he hired her, Ethan warned her he'd be actively seeking a qualified teacher for the spot he'd so unwillingly given her. *Who would be a better home ec teacher than the original?* Kristen might not know how to dress, but she could cook, sew, and sculpt milk cartons. How did Sunni ever think she could compete with that?

She was within inches of the door when Jennifer said, "Here's Ethan. Talk to him, Sunni."

"Talk to me about what?" Ethan asked.

Sunni was confused and humiliated. She didn't want to talk. She wanted to run. She shook her head. "I can't. I have to go."

Ethan caught her hand. "What is it? Is something wrong?"

Two chaperones selected that moment to wander over to talk to Ethan. He had no choice but to acknowledge them. Sunni used the interruption for her escape.

sixteen

Her mother looked up from her novel and frowned. "Hi, honey, what are you doing here? I wasn't expecting to see you tonight."

Sunni shrugged. "I just wanted to come home."

"Anytime—" Her mother narrowed her eyes to study Sunni. "Have you been crying?"

Sunni looked at her feet and shrugged again.

"Oh, honey." Her mother dropped the book and sprang to her feet to gather Sunni in her arms. "What's the matter?"

The warm embrace and maternal sympathy opened the floodgates. Sunni cried and cried.

"What in the world has upset you?" her mother asked when the worst of the storm had passed.

Sunni wasn't ready to go through the whole painful story. Since she'd never told her mother about her relationship with Ethan, she'd have to start her explanation at the beginning. She feared that if she relived the story her heart would break all over again.

She stepped back from her mother's arms and wiped away the tears with the back of her hand. "I'm not upset, really. Just tired. I put so much into the dance, and now it's over. I think I'm suffering from postparty letdown."

If her mother thought she'd shed an excessive amount of tears for a successful party, she didn't say so. "I'm sure you're right. What you need is a nice hot cup of tea. Why don't you come down to the kitchen with me, and you can tell me all about the dance while I fix you a cup?"

The kitchen was a huge room of gleaming stainless steel and white marble. Sunni sat on a stool at the island to watch her mother.

"So tell me about the dance," her mother said as she put the teakettle on to boil.

"It was lovely. We decorated the gym with red and silver metallic streamers and little white lights."

"I always like the twinkle lights," her mother said.

Sunni smiled. "I hired a DJ for the music. I used Bill Perkins, the same one we use at the country club."

Her mother nodded. "He does nice work. Although I personally think he plays the music much too loud."

Sunni chuckled. "It was loud. But the kids loved it."

"What did you do for refreshments?"

Sunni winced. "I asked volunteers to bring brownies and cookies and other finger foods. I thought I'd have my home ec students prepare the refreshments in class, but my principal specifically requested that we didn't. Something about the fire department being shorthanded for the holidays."

Her mother laughed. "Your principal sounds like a tease." She filled two bone china cups with boiling water and dropped a tea bag into each. She slid one of the cups and saucers across the counter to Sunni. "You're home awfully early. What time did the dance end?"

Sunni checked her watch. "Not for another hour."

Her mother frowned at her over her teacup. "Shouldn't you have stayed? It's a rather serious breach of etiquette for the hostess to leave her own party early."

"I wasn't the official hostess. Our principal is the host, and he'll be staying until the end."

They sipped their tea in silence.

"I've been meaning to tell you about a strange call I had the other day from Adele Cowper. I'm not sure I've ever mentioned her before. I haven't seen or talked to her in years. We went to school together and ran around a bit, but after we married, we went our separate ways. She married Ethan Harris about a year after I married your father."

Sunni's heart stopped. "Ethan Harris?" she choked out.

Her mother ignored her distress. "Yes. I didn't know him very well. His family was from Austin. They're big in oil."

"Oil? Like in oil wells?"

Her mother nodded. "That's where they made their money initially. Your father tells me they are more diversified now. Oil, computers. . .I can't remember all he told me." She sipped her tea. "Anyway, Adele called me the other day, out of the blue. It was so strange to hear from her after all this time. We had a nice chat though. She mentioned she has a son living in the area. He's a principal at one of the schools. She was so surprised to hear that my daughter was teaching at a local school and her principal's name was Harris. We had quite a laugh at the coincidence. I guess it's true what they say about it being a small world."

Sunni failed to see the humor. She was fixated on the most shocking revelation. "Ethan Harris comes from money?"

Her mother nodded. "To quote a tacky expression, the Harrises are filthy rich."

ॐ

Sunni tossed and turned till the early hours of the morning. Even the comfort of being tucked into her childhood bed failed to lull her to sleep. She had a lot to think about.

Lord, what went wrong?

Her dreams had turned upside down in the space of a few hours. It all happened so fast. One minute she was being lauded as a very special teacher, and the next minute she was a menace about to be replaced by Flamenco Red.

She couldn't decide whether she should be embarrassed, hurt, or mad. As she lay under the canopy, awaiting sleep that wouldn't come, she settled on a combination of all three.

She was embarrassed to death that Kristen repeated her unflattering nickname to the parents. She was humiliated that Ethan had begged Kristen to come back and that Sunni was likely out of a job just when she thought she was getting the hang of it. And it hurt like a blister from cheap shoes that the man she loved thought so little of her that he would denigrate her to her rival.

To cap off her hurt, Sunni was mad. Mad at Kristen for her spiteful remarks. Mad at Ethan for talking behind her back. And mad at herself for running out of the dance like a coward.

She should have stood her ground. She was Sunni Vanderclef. She might not possess mystical powers in the kitchen or swap craft ideas with Martha Stewart, but she had a unique God-given talent and the power to make a difference.

She had done so. Amanda Fenton wore less makeup and talked on the phone with friends. Seth met people's eyes when he talked, and—well, she didn't have any other success stories she could readily recall at three o'clock in the morning, but the fact was, she had made a positive contribution to Central Middle School. She wasn't much of a teacher, but she loved her students. That had to count for something.

Whether she should have marched up to Kristen at the dance and cataloged her own virtues to all and sundry was debatable. Blowing one's own horn was never in good taste.

Still, she should have stayed. Ethan might not owe her a job, but he owed her an explanation.

Father, she prayed as she drifted off at last, *I don't know what's going on, but You do. Help me trust You to do what's best.*

★

Sunni woke up tired and out of sorts. She wasn't depressed exactly, but she was definitely bummed out. It wouldn't take more than a chipped nail to push her into a full-blown funk.

She needed to call Ethan and get some answers, but she was afraid of what they might be.

Her mother must have sensed her mood. "I think we should do a little shopping this morning. Maybe have lunch at the country club."

"I don't know, Mom. I probably need to get home—"

Her mother gave her an eye roll that a middle schooler would be proud of. "It's the Christmas holidays. You don't have lesson plans due for three whole weeks. Take a day off. You've earned it."

"I don't know. . . ."

Her mother dangled a carrot in front of her vacillating daughter. "Sole Connection is having a sale."

Shoe sale. Nothing like a new pair of shoes to improve the mood and clear the mind. Finding a couple of really cute pairs on sale might well be enough of a boost that Sunni could overcome her fears and ask Ethan what she needed to know. Of course, they'd have to be pretty terrific shoes.

Sunni kept several changes of clothes at her parents' home so she didn't have to go home to get ready. She and her mother were on the road an hour after they agreed on shopping therapy.

While rummaging through her purse for a lipstick, Sunni noticed she had a message on her cell phone. "Sunni, it's Jennifer. Where are you? I called your house a half dozen times. I left you a message on your machine, but since I didn't know where you were, I thought I'd have more luck with your cell phone. You won't believe what happened at the dance. Ethan was upset after you left, and he asked me what was going on. I told him what Kristen said. He was livid. Oops! I bet I'm running out of time so I'll hurry. He said she was wrong. He said he's leaving Central. It's a secret. Call me."

Sunni replayed the message a second time to be sure she'd heard her friend correctly. *Ethan leaving Central?*

Her mother parked the car. "Come on, honey. Let's get inside. Karen Dunstan just pulled in, and I would hate for her to beat us to the bargains."

"You go ahead. I need to make one quick call."

Her mother hurried off in a restrained trot. Sunni dialed Jennifer's house. Six rings, no answer. "Jennifer, it's Sunni," she told the machine. "Call me on my cell."

She hung up and tried Ethan's home. No answer. She decided not to leave him a message. He didn't answer his cell either.

Sunni was too shocked to shop, even for sale shoes. *Ethan leaving?* She had to find out what was going on.

Her mother was seated in one of the pretty chintz club chairs with four boxes of shoes and a salesman at her feet. "Come here, Sunni. I'm so upset. I can't decide what I think about these shoes."

Her world was falling apart, and her mother was worried

about shoes? "They're only shoes," Sunni huffed in exasperation.

Her mother and the salesman turned to Sunni in horror. "Did you just say 'only shoes'?"

Sunni didn't have time for this. "I have to talk to Ethan." She spun around to leave and bumped into a solid wall of man. "Ethan?"

He clamped his hands on her arms to steady her. "Sunni, we need to talk."

"How did you find me?"

"Your mother's housekeeper told me you were here. She gave me very explicit instructions on how to find the place."

Sunni swung around to face her mother. "You left instructions on where to find us?"

Her mother's smile was sly though she tried for an innocent shrug. "You never know when someone will need to find us. You two run along. I can't concentrate on shoes when I'm eavesdropping."

Ethan extended his hand to her mother. "Mrs. Vanderclef, I'm Ethan Harris."

She took his hand and smiled. "It's a pleasure to meet you, Ethan. I had the nicest long talk with your mother the other day."

"You did? With my mother?"

She nodded. "We went to school together. Didn't she tell you?"

"She might have, but I don't remember her saying you two had kept in touch."

"It's a recent development." She waved Ethan and Sunni away. "Don't let me keep you. I'm sure you have lots to talk about. Sunni, don't worry about lunch. I'll ask Karen Dunstan instead."

Sunni followed Ethan out to his shiny black 4x4 parked

at the curb. He opened her door and helped her up before climbing in on the other side.

He turned sideways on the seat to face her. "Sunni, I owe you an apology."

"Just one?"

He took her hands in his, a stricken expression on his face. "I'm so sorry. Jennifer told me what Kristen said."

"Are you sorry I overheard Kristen calling me a menace or sorry I knew you must have told Kristen I was a menace?"

He was too overwrought to realize she was teasing. "Both! You have to believe I haven't thought of you as a menace in months. But I admit it was wrong of me to repeat it to her even when I did think you were a menace."

"Very wrong. And while we're dredging up your sins, shouldn't we talk about misleading me to believe you were poor? The way you condemned the evils of wealth, I figured you must have been raised under a bridge."

"I'm sorry. I know I came on pretty strong about you buying your way through life. The minute I heard the name *Vanderclef*, I had you pegged as a conscienceless socialite. It wasn't fair, but it's been my experience. The rich people I know are totally self-absorbed. My family is a prime example. They refuse to look beyond their own circles to see the needs they have the power to meet. But you're different, and I'm sorry it took me so long to realize it."

"You're forgiven."

He cupped her face in his hands. "Other than my faith, you are the single most precious thing in my life. I love you, Sunni."

"You do?"

"With all my heart. Not a second goes by that I don't think of you. I want us to be together all the time. I need you. I want you to marry me."

"Yes, I'll marry you—wait! How can you marry me? You're my boss." She frowned at him. "Is that why you're leaving Central?"

"Jennifer told you, huh?" He shrugged. "It's true. I've prayed about it, and I can't think of another solution to get us together."

"But, Ethan, what will you do?"

"One of the other junior high schools in the district has an opening for a history teacher. I spoke to the district superintendent yesterday, and he says the job is mine if I want it."

"You're giving up being a principal to go back to the classroom?"

"Yeah. It's okay. I like teaching history."

"But you've worked so hard for this. You've wanted to be a principal for so long."

"I'll still be working with the kids. That's the important thing."

"You would give up your life's dream for me?"

"Absolutely. Sunni, I love you. Without you, my dream seems pretty empty."

"Why didn't you ask me to give up my job?"

"Because you enjoy it."

She frowned up at him. "So let me get this right. The most respected principal in the district steps down so that an inept home ec teacher can keep her job?"

"You're not inept."

"I can't cook."

"You're improving. That bread your kids baked was edible."

"The loaves were flat as pancakes."

"Nobody's perfect."

"I think you are."

He gathered her into his arms for a long, satisfying kiss. She rested her head against his chest and sighed in pure contentment. "I quit."

His mind was obviously still on the kiss. "Hmm?"

"I said I quit. Consider this my two weeks' notice."

He pulled back to stare at her. "What are you talking about? Don't be ridiculous. You can't quit."

"I just did."

"But why? You don't have to do this. I'm going to another school. We can both work."

"No, thanks. I'm tired of teaching. It's cramping my social life."

"Sunni."

The way he dragged out her name then, as he used to when she was the menace and he was the beast principal, brought a smile to her face. She took his hands in hers and looked into his eyes. "Ethan, I believe your job at Central Middle is a sacred trust. I couldn't live with myself if I thought I came between you and what God called you to do. I only took the home ec job to prove I have some direction in my life. Nobody was more surprised than I was to discover I really do have a purpose. Now that I know I have something to contribute, I believe God will provide a place for me to serve."

"Sunni, I need to know you've given this a lot of thought. Are you absolutely sure you won't regret your decision later?"

"I've never been more sure of anything in my life." She leaned in to kiss him. "Now how do we stop the superintendent from moving you? Do you know where he lives?"

"Yeah, but I'd hate to drop in on him uninvited. It's

Saturday."

"Trust me. This is one interruption he'll welcome."

❧

The superintendent clapped Ethan on the back. "Ethan, I can't tell you how happy I am that you've changed your mind about giving up Central Middle School."

"You can thank Sunni."

"You are an extraordinary woman, Ms. Vanderclef. I can see why Ethan was so determined to have you."

"Thank you, sir."

"The only unsatisfactory part of this whole business is the potential loss of such a positive influence on our young people. Ethan keeps us posted with the doings of your club, and I'm very impressed. You've made real inroads into building the self-esteem of the students at Central."

"Thank you. They're great kids. It's been a privilege to work with them."

"Tell me, Ms. Vanderclef—if I were able to come up with a way to keep you on district staff, would you be interested?"

"I'm not sure I understand."

"I'll have to clear it with the board, of course, but I'd like to propose we hire you as a consultant of sorts. To come up with a friendship-building curriculum you could present in the form of special assemblies and seminars at each of our schools. In addition, I'd like you to draw up detailed blueprints for creating Clubs on other campuses. You could instruct each school's faculty on how to implement the Club in their school. Once established, you would serve as district liaison to each of the Clubs, as an advisor to the school sponsors. Does that sound like something you'd be interested in?"

"Yes, sir."

"Is there any way Sunni could continue on as the sponsor for Central's Club?" Ethan asked. "At least until the end of the year?"

The superintendent smiled. "I insist."

❧

May was always a big month at Central. The end of school meant final exams, parties, and graduation. And this year, to make a big month bigger, a wedding.

While waiting for the final assembly to begin, the faculty and members of the Club who attended the society event of the year were still buzzing about last weekend's fairytale wedding of the principal and the home ec teacher.

"Good afternoon and welcome to Central Middle School's commencement," Ethan said from the podium in the center of the stage. "We're going to keep things brief so my wife and I can get on to our honeymoon."

Sunni, sitting in the third row of the auditorium, laughed along with the others.

"We'll begin the program with the presentation of academic awards."

Following the academic awards came the athletic awards and finally the attendance awards. As the last student stepped from the stage, Ethan said, "It is a tradition here at Central to select one teacher each year as Teacher of the Year."

Sunni noticed all heads turning toward Kristen Hobart. She thought Kristen was looking mighty smug.

"This teacher," Ethan continued, "as voted upon by faculty and students, is the teacher who best exemplifies excellence in the classroom. I'm very proud to announce this year's Teacher of the Year, Jennifer Stanton."

Sunni clapped till her palms felt raw.

After Jennifer's brief acceptance speech, Ethan returned to the podium. "Now, before we are dismissed for the year, our PTA president, Mrs. Rhoades, has asked to make a special presentation."

Mrs. Rhoades joined him at the microphone. "Thank you, Mr. Harris. The PTA would like to present a new award this year. The award, as voted on by PTA members, will go to the volunteer or faculty member we feel has made the greatest contribution to the middle school over the year. With so many wonderful parents and teachers to choose from, the choice was a difficult one. But when we looked at the facts, one person stood out as a clear leader."

She continued, "Today's recipient, though new to our school, has loved her way into the hearts of students and staff. Through her tireless efforts, our children are better, happier people. Let me introduce this year's recipient of the PTA Sunshine Award—Sunni Vanderclef Harris. From all of us at Central Middle School, I'd like to say, thanks for making a difference."

A Letter to Our Readers

Dear Reader:

In order that we might better contribute to your reading enjoyment, we would appreciate your taking a few minutes to respond to the following questions. We welcome your comments and read each form and letter we receive. When completed, please return to the following:

Fiction Editor
Heartsong Presents
PO Box 721
Uhrichsville, Ohio 44683

1. Did you enjoy reading *Miss Menace* by Nancy Lavo?
   ❑ Very much! I would like to see more books by this author!
   ❑ Moderately. I would have enjoyed it more if

   _____

   _____

   _____

2. Are you a member of **Heartsong Presents**? ❑ Yes ❑ No
   If no, where did you purchase this book? _____

   _____

3. How would you rate, on a scale from 1 (poor) to 5 (superior), the cover design? _____

4. On a scale from 1 (poor) to 10 (superior), please rate the following elements.

   ____ Heroine   ____ Plot
   ____ Hero   ____ Inspirational theme
   ____ Setting   ____ Secondary characters

5. These characters were special because _____
_____
_____

6. How has this book inspired your life? _____
_____
_____

7. What settings would you like to see covered in future
Heartsong Presents books? _____
_____
_____

8. What are some inspirational themes you would like to see
treated in future books? _____
_____
_____

9. Would you be interested in reading other **Heartsong
Presents** titles? ❏ Yes ❏ No

10. Please check your age range:
    ❏ Under 18   ❏ 18-24
    ❏ 25-34   ❏ 35-45
    ❏ 46-55   ❏ Over 55

Name _____
Occupation _____
Address _____
City, State, Zip _____

fresh-brewed love

4 stories in 1

Four women find grounds for love where romance blossoms over cups of coffee. Can these women make the right decisions when it comes to love? Authors include Susan K. Downs, Anita Higman, DiAnn Mills, and Kathleen Y'Barbo.

Contemporary, paperback, 352 pages, 5³⁄₁₆" x 8"

Heart♥ng

Any 12 Heartsong Presents titles for only $27.00*

CONTEMPORARY ROMANCE IS CHEAPER BY THE DOZEN!

Buy any assortment of twelve *Heartsong Presents* titles and save 25% off the already discounted price of $2.97 each!

*plus $2.00 shipping and handling per order and sales tax where applicable.

HEARTSONG PRESENTS TITLES AVAILABLE NOW:

(If ordering from this page, please remember to include it with the order form.)

Presents

Great Inspirational Romance at a Great Price!

Heartsong Presents books are inspirational romances in contemporary and historical settings, designed to give you an enjoyable, spirit-lifting reading experience. You can choose wonderfully written titles from some of today's best authors like Hannah Alexander, Andrea Boeshaar, Yvonne Lehman, Tracie Peterson, and many others.

When ordering quantities less than twelve, above titles are $2.97 each.
Not all titles may be available at time of order.